The
ANIMALS
—of—
FARTHING
WOOD

Through Battle and Storm

The
ANIMALS
—of—
FARTHING
WOOD

Colin Dann

RED FOX

A Red Fox Book

Published by Random House Children's Books
20 Vauxhall Bridge Road, London SW1V 2SA

A division of Random House UK Ltd
London Melbourne Sydney Auckland
Johannesburg and agencies throughout the world

1 3 5 7 9 10 8 6 4 2

First published by Red Fox 1995

Set in Bembo by Intype, London
Printed and bound in Great Britain by
Cox and Wyman Ltd, Reading, Berkshire
RANDOM HOUSE UK Limited Reg. No. 954009

ISBN 0 09 950081 7

CONTENTS

Part I

IN THE PATH OF THE STORM

PROLOGUE

One early morning in March Whistler the heron stood by the stream in White Deer Park looking for fish. It was raining. It had been raining for too long. The raindrops disturbed the water, making it hard for Whistler to see the fish. He had been standing so long he had begun to doze.

From the woodland near the stream the towering figure of the Great Stag came to drink. Ignoring Whistler, he bent his head to the water. Whistler noticed movement and turned to watch. The Great Stag finished drinking and stood upright. Suddenly his body began to shake violently. His legs gave way and he crashed on to his side. The stag's body twitched once or twice, then lay still. Whistler hurriedly flew to him. One close look told the heron the stag was dead.

Miserable, Whistler flew to find his companions from Farthing Wood. The Great Stag had been a friend to them all since their arrival in the Park and the heron needed to share his awful news. Eventually he saw Badger busy collecting fresh bedding for his sett. The familiar sound of Whistler's damaged wing made the old creature look up.

'Hallo, Whistler! More rain, more rain. Everything's waterlogged. It's difficult to find dry – ' He broke off as he saw the bird's look of anguish. 'Why, whatever's the matter?' he asked.

'I have terrible news,' Whistler replied. 'The Great Stag is dead. I saw him die. It was horribly sudden.' He described what he had seen.

Badger was stunned, unable to find words. Finally he muttered, 'Dreadful. Quite dreadful.' He began to back away. 'I must get this bedding underground,' he murmured.

'I'll go,' said Whistler. 'I'll tell the others.'

Badger's thoughts were full of the sad event as he tried to make his sett comfortable. How would the Great Stag's death change life in the Park?

The other animals wondered the same thing when they heard the news. They gathered to consider the loss of a much revered friend.

'It's the end of the old order,' said Fox.

'Who'll take his place?' asked Leveret the young hare. 'There will be a new leader, won't there?'

'Only after a battle,' Owl said. 'There's bound to be rivalry between the stags.'

They knew the fighting wouldn't occur until the breeding season and that was months away. They took a final look at the body of the aged leader of the deer herd as it rocked gently with the current of the stream.

4

CHAPTER ONE

Toad and Adder came out of hibernation to find the Park still soaked by the rain. This suited the water-loving Toad, but Adder wanted somewhere dry and warm. It wasn't long before they heard about the Great Stag's death. Owl told them. Toad and Adder looked glum.

'Whistler saw it happen by the stream,' Owl said. 'After the Stag had drunk from it. And there seem to be very few fish about at present. There's something odd about that stream.'

Adder and Toad parted, since Adder was eager to find a dry spot. She had a good idea where she might find one. 'Badger's sett,' she hissed to herself. 'That's bound to be warm and comfortable.'

There were many births that spring amongst the Farthing Wood animals. Fox and Vixen had their first great grandchildren. A male cub was born who reminded them vividly of their son Bold who had left White Deer Park and not survived. This cub was called Plucky.

'He's the image of Bold at that age,' Vixen breathed. 'It'll be such fun to see him grow up.'

Of the original members of the Farthing Wood band only Badger and Owl hadn't found mates. Badger was very old and forgetful but the younger animals loved him dearly. However, they sometimes teased Owl who had not yet reached old age and yet was still on her own. Two of the younger foxes, now parents themselves, couldn't resist winding her up.

'Poor old Owl – she couldn't find a mate,' Rusty called beneath her roost.

'Are there no single males left for you?' Pace chuckled.

'Stop annoying me,' replied Owl, crossly. 'Haven't you got anything better to do?'

'Haven't *you*?' Rusty teased.

'Think of all those gentlemen owls dying to get to know the famous Owl from Farthing Wood,' Pace continued.

'They must be patient and wait then, mustn't they?' Owl snapped. She knew it was a mistake to react to the foxes' taunts but it was impossible not to do so.

'Wait for what?'

'For me to choose to get acquainted,' she answered pompously.

'Oh. Listen to that, Rusty. I always thought it was they who had chosen not to become acquainted with Owl?'

'Must be, Pace. After all, she is the only unmated one of the Farthing Wood elders.'

'I am NOT!' screeched Owl. 'What about Badger?'

'Poor old Badger?' Rusty cried. 'You can hardly count – ' He broke off as he saw his mother, Charmer, approaching.

'What's going on?' Charmer demanded, sensing mischief.

'They're mocking me,' Owl complained.

'Whatever for?'

'It's only because she has no mate,' Pace explained. 'Just a bit of fun.'

'It's no business of yours whether Owl has a mate or not,' Charmer scolded the youngsters. 'You should be more respectful to your elders. Leave her in peace and tend to your own business.' She lowered her voice. 'It's not nice to scoff at another creature's bad luck.'

Pace and Rusty looked ashamed. They hadn't intended any harm. But Owl had, unfortunately, heard Charmer's last remark and was humiliated. Bad luck? Well, she'd show them! She was furious. In a temper she flapped away over the tree-tops, not perching again until she was well hidden from any further cruel teasers. Her feelings were hurt badly and she knew she must do something to prove the young foxes wrong. The trouble was, it would be all but impossible to find another single owl in

White Deer Park now. It was too late into the season.

'Nothing else for it,' she told herself. 'I'll have to go outside the Park.' She felt some relief. At least then none of her old companions – or new ones – would be able to keep a check on her.

CHAPTER TWO

It was a while before Owl's absence was noticed. Mossy, Mole's son, tunnelled his way into Badger's sett. Badger was in a bad mood. Adder seemed to have set up home in his sett, even though the wet weather was long over. So the old creature didn't at first listen to Mossy's message, he was grumbling to himself so much. 'Wants her bedding provided,' he was muttering about the snake. 'Just like her cheek.'

Mossy didn't wish to talk about Adder. 'Have you seen Owl recently?' he asked.

'What? Owl? No, I haven't,' Badger grunted irritably.

'Weasel thinks she's disappeared, after the young foxes' badgering.' Mossy tittered nervously.

Badger wasn't amused by the pun. 'What's all this about?'

Mossy explained. 'They've been teasing her. Because of her still being on her own.'

'Nothing wrong with being alone. *I'd* enjoy it,' Badger said pointedly.

'That's not what I meant,' said Mossy and explained further.

'I see,' said Badger. 'Poor old Owl. Driven out like that!'

Adder had overheard everything. 'The bird's gone searching for a mate,' she guessed. 'How absurd at her age. She's not exactly a glossy-plumed youngster.'

'We must do something,' Badger declared. 'Bring her back. I'll speak to Fox.' He left the sett, followed by Mossy.

Adder mocked them as they went. 'You'll need to sprout wings,' she hissed. But the idea of a search for Owl reminded her of one she had considered making herself. She had been wondering if Sinuous the male adder had returned to his usual summer-time haunts. It was a sunny day and she decided to slither out.

Fox and Vixen had been watching a group of white stags who at this season kept themselves apart from the female deer. There was one large animal, a proud and commanding beast whose antlers already had grown to a greater size than his companions'. He was known as Trey.

'Look at the way he carries himself,' Fox remarked. 'I wonder how we'll get along with him?'

'Yes, he seems to know he has no rivals,' Vixen replied. 'I only hope he doesn't decide to move in on our corner of the Park.'

'We'll keep ourselves to ourselves,' Fox vowed. 'That can't cause any trouble.'

10

By the time Badger reached Fox and Vixen's earth, Owl was far away. She had met no-one in the woods and copses close to the Reserve and so had flown on further. Before long the landscape began to seem very familiar to her. She had travelled over the same countryside in the other direction during the Farthing Wood animals' long journey to safety in the Nature Reserve. She perched in an oak tree and rested. In a while she was asleep and dreaming about her old life in Farthing Wood. She awoke with a start and a sudden idea.

'Why don't I retrace the entire journey? Back to our old home? There must be a spot with a few trees still standing. What a story I'd have to tell everyone on my return! And somewhere on the way I'll be bound to find that special companion . . .' She was delighted with her new plan and set off at once.

During the night Owl hunted and ate hungrily. She knew she would need all her strength. She flew onward and, recognizing a landmark in the distance, aimed for it as dawn approached. This was a church tower she had sheltered in before, on that other great journey.

'This'll suit very well,' she decided, landing on a stone sill. But, just as she began to relax, a colony of bats who roosted in the belfry, returned in force. They were angry at Owl's presence and tried to dislodge her. They flew all around her, zipping past her head and dive-bombing her from all angles.

'Stop it!' she cried. 'I'm no threat to you. I only want to sleep through the daylight like you.'

But the bats weren't satisfied with her words. 'Fly away,' they shrilled in their tiny squeaky voices. 'Leave our roost!'

Owl was at her wits' end because she needed to rest. The bats disturbed her but at the same time she marvelled at their wonderful flying skills.

'I don't want to eat you,' she cried. 'My stomach's full already. Besides, I couldn't catch you if I tried.'

The bats quietened and began to hang themselves upside down from the rafters which they gripped tightly with their toes. A hundred bat eyes watched Owl warily until she fell asleep.

The next evening Owl left the belfry before the bats stirred. The lights of a nearby town beckoned. She flew high overhead, then looked for another land-mark. The distant hum of traffic reminded her of the motorway the Farthing Wood animals had had to cross. She flew towards the sound and, sure enough, there it was. The road was lit by the head-lamps of a stream of vehicles which streaked past like shooting stars. She perched in an ash tree and watched. She had already covered a good distance from White Deer Park.

CHAPTER THREE

Fox and Vixen were as worried as Badger was about Owl's disappearance.

'To think of one of the Farthing Wood elders feeling herself forced out of the Park,' Fox said indignantly. 'Pace and Rusty should have a good telling off.'

'But Fox, the point is, what can we do to get Owl back?' Badger groaned. 'She's so proud, she won't return until she's managed to find a mate.'

'Did you say that Weasel knows something about all this?' Fox asked.

'Apparently,' Badger answered.

'Then I think we should have a word with her.'

There was no difficulty in finding Weasel, but she didn't seem very eager to help. 'What can I do?' she asked. 'Owl's gone off in a huff. She'll soon recover from it and then she'll be back.'

'You're right, of course,' Fox admitted.

'But we can't desert Owl, can we?' Vixen pleaded.

'We haven't,' Weasel replied. 'She's deserted us. Really, there's nothing to be done but wait. You must see that it's impossible for us to go in search of a bird.'

'It's awful to think of her out there in danger,' Badger said.

'She has wings, hasn't she?' Weasel returned. 'Those are her – ' She stopped suddenly. The others followed her glance. She had spied Trey, the big stag, coming towards them.

When he was close Trey spoke in a harsh voice. 'You're some of the old travellers who came here from another place, I believe?'

'That's correct,' Fox answered.

'You realize we didn't invite you here?'

'What do you mean? And who's "we"?'

'The herd, of course, of which I am the natural leader.'

'Some of the stags might argue with that,' Fox retorted.

'Who can argue with *me, Trey*?' the big stag demanded. 'Have you ever seen antlers like these?'

'Yes,' Vixen replied coolly. 'The Great White Stag had finer ones.'

Trey glared at her. 'He was a fine beast,' he had to admit. 'But his day's over and now things will change.'

'We'd like to know about these changes,' Badger spoke for all, 'since we live here too.'

'Exactly,' Trey replied. 'We've allowed you to, whereas this Nature Reserve was set aside for us alone. We gave it its name: White Deer Park. This area of land could never have been reserved for common creatures such as you.'

Fox was very angry. 'You are arrogant,' he said. 'I too have authority and am respected here. And I'd like to see you brought down to earth.'

'The only thing you'll see,' Trey remarked loftily, 'is that I am now Lord of the Reserve. You must all stay in your corner of the Park. I want no interference with the herd's grazing. Otherwise we won't allow you to stay here any longer.' He turned and stepped away as though he had better things to do.

For a moment the friends were speechless. Then Fox said, 'We're going to have trouble with that animal. "Lord of the Reserve" indeed! Well, at least it gives us an idea of his intentions.'

'The thing is, what do we do about him?' Weasel asked. 'I'm not going to confine myself to one small area as that stag says. Why should I?'

'It won't make much difference to me,' Badger remarked. 'I rarely wander far these days.'

'We'll continue to live here as we choose,' Fox said determinedly. 'Trey's words may be all bluster.'

'I think we should warn the smaller animals, though,' Vixen said. 'Trey mentioned the herd's grazing. We don't want the rabbits and hares to fall foul of him.'

'You're quite right,' Fox agreed. 'I'll tell Leveret to be cautious and he can spread the word.'

There was no more to discuss and the friends parted. However, Fox was too late to warn Leveret.

The young hare, over on the other side of the Park, was busy munching the juicy growths of grass which were thick and lush because of all the spring rain. He had no fear of the deer herd. Previously the deer had always been friendly. So he had no knowledge that he was at any risk, and the sudden appearance of Trey didn't bother him.

But Trey's huge head loomed in front of Leveret. The stag's expression was definitely unfriendly. Leveret stopped nibbling. Trey stamped the ground impatiently with a front hoof like a bull about to charge. Leveret realized the danger and leapt up and bounded away through the grasses with Trey in hot pursuit. Luckily, Leveret could outrun any creature and he was soon well away from the stag. But he was badly frightened. He ran across Friendly, Fox and Vixen's son, almost colliding with him.

'Hey, what's the hurry?' Friendly called cheerfully.

Leveret calmed down, then explained. 'There's a mad creature amongst the deer herd. He charged at me without warning!'

Friendly recognized the culprit. He'd heard all about his parents' encounter. 'Oh, you mean Trey. The mighty new Lord of the Reserve. He's the Great Stag's successor, or so *he* thinks. Only he wants to dominate all of us as well as the deer herd.'

'But – but – the deer were always friendly in the old days,' Leveret spluttered.

'Well, these are new days, Leveret,' said Friendly.

16

'The old order has passed. And it seems we're to accept it — or go.'

CHAPTER FOUR

Meanwhile Owl's journey continued. She occasion-
ally heard another owl call to its mate, which
reminded her why she had left the Park. However
she still hadn't met any other lone owls. She flew
over the fox-hunting land where Vixen nearly lost
her life, pausing there only to eat. By the next dawn
she was on the banks of the river which she and
her friends had crossed, with mixed fortunes, on the
way to White Deer Park. She rested during that day
in a hollow oak.

The next evening she flew over the river and
steered her course for the copse where the Farthing
Wood animals had been entertained by the local
rooks. The speed with which she was covering the
distance was in marked contrast to the animals' long
trek. Then they had had to travel at the pace of the
slowest, such as Toad and the voles and mice. Owl
was astonished by her rapid progress now.

Yet beyond the copse the way was not as clear so
she rested again. The next night she set off with a
picture in her mind of an orchard, a marsh, a road
and rows of houses. That was the route back if the

landscape hadn't changed. But of course it had, and Owl couldn't get her bearings.

'I shall have to seek help,' she told herself. She headed for a squirrel's drey.

The squirrels weren't pleased to see an owl in their tree, but Owl calmed them down by asking for directions. 'Do you know a place called Farthing Wood? It can't be far from here.'

'No wood anywhere round here,' the mother squirrel replied, 'otherwise *we'd* be living in it.'

'I've heard the name,' the father squirrel said. 'There was a tale attached to it. What was it? Some animals got together to help each other in some way.'

Owl perked up. 'Yes, yes,' she said. 'That's the place. Which way would it have been from here?'

'Hm. Must be where the human dwellings have spread,' came the answer.

Owl was overjoyed. 'Yes! That's it!'

'Well, if you fly over the hill, you'll see plenty of buildings. They're all around there.'

'I'm most grateful,' Owl hooted and she waited no longer. And over the hill, below her she saw the bright lights of houses and streets.

'There,' she whispered to herself with a gulp. 'I'm home.'

But she wasn't. Not quite.

Since the death of the Great Stag, the Farthing Wood animals had kept away from the stream. Whistler could no longer find live fish and there were more signs that something was wrong with the water-course. The heron discovered the dead bodies of small creatures such as water-voles lying by its side as well as some young coots dead in their nest. He tried to find a clue to these strange deaths in the water but could see nothing.

But there were plenty of puddles of rainwater available as well as the Pond to drink from. However, it was only a matter of time before one of the Farthing Wood animals would be confronted by Trey at the Pond. The foxes roamed farthest afield and the young Plucky was the first animal to be challenged by Trey as he drank.

'This Pond is the herd's drinking place,' the stag warned.

'Yes, it's a very convenient place for us all,' Plucky replied confidently.

'Oh, is it?' Trey returned. 'We'll see about that. My herd needs plenty of fresh water so in future you and the other lesser creatures will not be allowed to drink here.'

Plucky was amazed. 'But there's enough for everyone here,' he argued.

'Not if there should be a dry spell,' Trey replied. 'So remember what I've said.'

Plucky lost no time in passing the message on to the senior foxes.

'What a nerve,' Fox growled. 'Dictating to us!'

'He doesn't speak for the herd,' Vixen pointed out. 'The hinds are as friendly as ever.'

'Nevertheless, we need to meet with the others and talk about this,' Fox said. 'Plucky, take the word round. The Hollow. Dusk tomorrow.'

The next night the Farthing Wood elders gathered in their traditional meeting-place.

'Well, we know the situation,' said Fox. 'Has anyone any suggestions?'

'Call his bluff,' Weasel answered promptly. 'Like we said before.'

'Yes,' Fox agreed. 'We shall ignore his threats. But you know, what we need is a champion.'

'A champion?' Toad echoed. 'A champion what?'

'A champion fool, I would guess, if he tried to meddle with that stag,' Adder hissed.

'No, let me explain,' Fox chuckled. 'I mean a champion from amongst the deer herd. In other words, a challenger.'

'How do we find one?' Badger asked. 'The other stags are all under Trey's rule.'

'Wait until the rut. Things will be different then,' Fox reminded him. 'Even the Great Stag had to fight off challengers at those times. And in the meantime, all of us can stir them up a little.'

'Stir them up?' Leveret repeated. 'What can we do?'

'Well, you know, drop a hint here and there

amongst the males. Set them on. We'll tell them Trey intends to drive all rivals from the Park.'

CHAPTER FIVE

Owl was bewildered by the mass of buildings spread before her. All at once she wondered why she had come here. There was no Farthing Wood any more. This expanse of concrete, brick and glass, with its countless lights, had replaced the lush trees and bushes. If she hadn't managed to find a companion on her flight here, how on earth could she hope to do so in this man-made world? Her immediate problem was to find a roost. There seemed to be no trees at all of any size, only slender saplings with twigs for branches which the humans had planted along the roads. She flew closer, her courage ebbing fast. In one building, high up, there was a dark hole which offered shelter and a hideaway, at least for a while. Owl could see nothing better and it did offer an escape from the noise and lights. But Owl didn't realize that it was in fact an open window into a dark attic. She flew through the opening and perched on a shelf at the far end of the room. There was a snug gap here between two rows of books. Owl settled herself, listening to the distant sounds of humans below. They seemed to pose no threat and eventually she dozed.

During the night a strong breeze began to blow against the window so that it gradually closed. Owl awoke to her danger too late. As she flew towards the window in a panic a particularly strong gust blew it quite closed. She was trapped. She squeezed herself between the books again and tried to think what she must do.

When daylight returned she was still there. The gathering noise outside made her shrink back with alarm. But at the same time she knew she couldn't stay where she was. Owl noticed the door to the attic room was open and this was her only escape route. Before she could summon up the courage to make a move a black cat, who had sensed her presence, padded into the attic.

'*There* you are,' the cat said, staring at Owl. 'How did you get in?'

'I flew in, of course,' Owl blustered. 'Then the hole closed up and – '

'You can't fly through glass,' the cat finished for her. 'I see. Well, you can't stay there. We don't allow vermin in the house. There used to be a lot of mice until I dealt with them. Are you vermin?'

The Farthing Wood Owl drew herself up. 'How dare you!' she screeched. 'I *hunt* vermin. I *eat* vermin. I – I – ' She launched herself furiously from the shelf and out of the open door, narrowly missing a little ginger-haired boy who had come in search of the cat.

The boy screamed and Owl banked sharply as she swooped down the staircase. 'Daddy! A bird! A bird in the loft!' the little boy shrieked.

There was another open door on the landing. Owl went through it, looking for a way out of the house. There was no window open here. It was a girl's bedroom and the owner, who was sitting at her dressing-table, now shrieked with her brother as Owl skimmed her hair.

Poor Owl veered from right to left as the father hastily arrived and tried to knock her to the floor.

'Don't hit it, Dad, please,' the girl begged. 'It just wants to get out.'

The man went to the window to open it, but Owl ducked past him and out to the landing and another staircase. She flew down to the hall and then into another room where a small window was open offering an escape at last. She zoomed towards it, with the cries of the family ringing in her ears. Squirming through the window, she soared upwards, gulping in air and stretching her wings to their utmost. She was free again!

She flew on over house-tops, over blocks of flats until suddenly a lone beech tree, a massive thing, beckoned her to its leafy embrace. And now Owl knew for certain that beneath all the concrete, the man-made blocks of brick and tile, was what had once been Farthing Wood. She recognized the beech tree at once as the very tree below which the Farthing Wood animals had gathered at the start of their long trek to a new home. And this great tree was all that the humans had allowed to survive of the old woodland. Owl flew gladly into its lofty boughs, relieved to be hidden and safe once more.

CHAPTER SIX

Owl stayed put during the daylight. She was hungry and thought about what the black cat had said about mice. There must be some around still for her. If anyone could find them, Owl could. She thought about her friends in White Deer Park. Time and distance had healed her wounds and she felt home-sick.

As dusk fell Owl sought water. Having quenched her thirst, she set about catching her supper. She sought mice in the gardens, around sheds, under hedgerows. And she found them. After a while she became aware of another hunter after the same prey. She caught a glimpse of the bird pouncing to make a kill close to where she was flying. She returned to the beech tree with her latest victim. As she ate she could see the other bird flying in her direction. It was another owl.

The second bird landed on a branch of the beech to eat its prey. Abruptly it turned and spoke, 'How long have you been hunting in this area?'

A male owl! She hardly dared to hope. 'I haven't

been here for a long time,' she answered breathlessly. 'But I know all about Farthing Wood.'

'Oh, Farthing Wood!' the other bird mocked. 'You mean Farthinghurst, don't you? That's what it's called now.'

'Farthinghurst?'

'Yes, the Wood's long gone.'

'I can see that!' Owl exclaimed irritably. 'But this tree at least was a part of it. It's all that remains.'

'How do you know so much?' the male owl asked her.

'It's a long story,' Owl answered. 'I was born and fledged in Farthing Wood. But I left when the men came to destroy it.'

'I see. Well, I too was born on its fringes amid the roar of men's machinery. I stayed on here when the last of the Wood disappeared. There was plenty of food – an abundance of mice.'

'So I've heard.'

'Not so many now. But enough for a lone owl. Although not so lone now,' he joked. 'I saw you sheltering here in the daytime. You didn't notice me.'

'I was exhausted,' Owl explained and described her adventure in the loft.

'It was a mistake to enter a human dwelling,' the male bird told her. 'I steer clear of them.'

'Quite right,' Owl agreed. 'But it was nothing next to the adventures I had when I left Farthing Wood.'

28

'Tell me about them.'

Owl did so eagerly. She related the entire story of the animals of Farthing Wood's journey. Her companion listened with rapt attention.

'Well, that's quite a tale, Owl,' he said afterwards. 'And so you all made your homes in White Deer Park?'

'Yes. And I shall soon return there.'

'It's so strange for a bird to make friends with mammals and even a reptile.'

'True comrades, all of them,' Owl replied loyally. 'Don't you ever get lonely?'

'I hadn't thought about it before,' the male bird murmured. 'But now I see the advantage of having friends.'

'I could be a friend,' Owl offered hopefully.

'Perhaps you already are.'

'I must have a name to call you, then.'

'Well, give me one.'

Owl considered. 'How about Hollow?'

'Hm. Hollow,' the male owl tried the name out. 'Yes, I think I rather like it.'

Owl was pleased. Now she was glad she had flown this far after all. Fate had brought her to the last surviving tree, the symbol of Farthing Wood, and here she had found Hollow.

'Are you going to roost on that branch?' Hollow asked her.

'Yes.'

'Then I'll join you,' he said and fluttered over. 'Friends must stick together, mustn't they?'

The two owls became firm friends. Each night they hunted together and shared their catch of mice. Hollow enjoyed having company, while Owl could think of nothing but of how she could persuade him to fly back with her to White Deer Park. But Hollow seemed so content that she hesitated to make the suggestion.

Time passed and Owl decided she really shouldn't stay around Farthinghurst any longer. Mice were in short supply and Owl and Hollow had flown all over the estate one night without much luck. Owl was weary and wanted to return to their roost. Hollow, however, wanted to try one last spot. He was younger and didn't tire so soon. 'You go back if you like,' he said.

'Oh no,' Owl replied, not wishing her age to become too noticeable. 'If you want to go on, I'm game.'

'See those new man-dwellings over there?' Hollow asked, beginning to fly towards them. 'I'm sure I saw something move on the ground.'

'I'll go ahead and look,' Owl offered, hoping her new eagerness would impress the male bird. She was flying swiftly ahead when she blundered into some almost invisible netting. Owl was entangled and crashed down with a thump on to an unfinished wet cement driveway which the netting had protected. Owl struggled and struggled to free herself, her talons and wings getting covered with the sticky mix. She managed to get airborne but her wing feathers felt tacky and uncomfortable. She felt out of balance too, as though one side of her body was heavier than the other. Meanwhile Hollow had pounced on the mouse.

'Hunting's over for me tonight,' Owl gasped. 'Look at my talons!' She bumbled her way back to the beech in a zig-zag way, finding it impossible to fly straight. She landed awkwardly; her plastered claws were unable to grasp the perch properly.

Hollow returned and laid the dead mouse at her feet. Owl looked gloomy as he ate. In the moonlight Hollow could see the sorry state his companion was in. 'I'm so sorry you fell,' he said.

'So am I,' Owl muttered. 'I'm afraid you'll have to do the hunting for both of us from now on. I feel I couldn't fly now to save my life.'

'I'll go and find more food,' Hollow said. 'You must rest.'

In his absence Owl tried to flap her wings but only lost her balance. She hastily righted herself and remained still. She felt weighed down and almost rigid. The cement was hardening, encasing her wings.

'I don't know what I've done,' she moaned. She was frightened. 'I think I may never be able to fly again!'

CHAPTER SEVEN

In White Deer Park Owl's friends were taking care to keep out of the way of Trey. They continued to visit the Pond but only if the coast was clear. Fox meanwhile planted the idea in the minds of the other white stags that Trey meant to drive them out. Some were indignant, others disbelieving. The more timid males dismissed the idea. 'He wouldn't bother with me. I'm no threat,' was their response. But many stags resented Trey's conceit and Fox felt he had prepared the ground for future challenges.

The summer sun shone on the Park and dried out the last of the pools of rainwater close to Badger's sett.

'Oh dear,' said thirsty Badger. 'It's a long way from here to the Pond for my old legs. The stream's so much nearer. If only I could drink there.' He thought for a moment. 'Maybe I can after all,' he muttered. 'How do we know there's anything wrong with it?' He was still in doubt. 'Oh well,' he decided, 'I can go and have a look at the water anyway.'

He shambled off to the stream. He stared at the

water and then shuffled down the bank to smell it. His powerful nose couldn't detect anything wrong. 'Perhaps I'll just go a little way to see if anyone else is drinking,' he told himself.

Sure enough he soon heard sounds of lapping. He hurried forward. A rabbit had been drinking and, timidly, began running away. 'Don't go,' he called. 'It's only old Badger.' It paused at the top of the bank.

'Notice anything strange about the water?' Badger asked. 'Funny taste at all?'

'No.'

'Oh, that's good.' Badger sighed with relief and bent to take a couple of mouthfuls.

'Trey's not around, is he?' the rabbit asked nervously.

'No.'

'He drove me off, you know, from the Pond. I had to come here instead. The others said it was a risk but – '

'A risk?' Badger gulped.

'Well, there have been stories, haven't there? Creatures dying here.' The rabbit coughed.

Badger was alarmed. 'What's the matter?' he barked edgily.

'Nothing – a sort of tickle.'

'A – tickle?' Badger muttered.

'Yes. Sort of a hot feeling in my throat.'

'You'd better go back to your warren,' Badger advised.

'I will, but I must have another drink first. I'm so dry again.'

'Don't!' Badger called. He was fearful now. But the rabbit was desperate and drank deeply. Badger waited for something awful to happen. The rabbit turned and began to run away. Badger followed. The rabbit was soon far ahead. Badger tried to hurry and suddenly he saw the little animal slow down, its body overcome by a spasm of shaking. Then it fell. As he came up he knew only too well it was dead.

'The stream's a killer,' he whispered in horror. 'And I've drunk from it!' He stood stock still. What should he do? Now he felt thirstier than ever. Just like the rabbit! 'I may be too late but I must get to the Pond,' he urged himself. 'I must drink my fill of clean water. Wash out the poisoned stuff!' He glanced once more at the dead rabbit and hurried on.

By the time he reached the Pond it was nearly light. He pushed through the reeds and lowered his muzzle thankfully, taking great gulps of water. There was a sound of pounding hooves.

'Stop!' bellowed a deep voice.

Badger looked up. Trey was galloping towards him.

'You've no right here!' thundered Trey. 'I've warned you animals.'

Badger's thirst overcame any fear of Trey. He continued to drink.

34

'Do you defy me?' boomed the stag, lowering his antlers.

'I have to drink where I can,' Badger answered reasonably.

'Very well, as you're so determined to have this water, I'll help you to reach it,' Trey told him angrily. He prepared to butt Badger in the rump and hurl him into the Pond. He took a few steps back and took aim. Just as he prepared to charge a third animal, Plucky, appeared on the scene and at once saw Badger's danger. He raced up and, as Trey began to charge, bit deep into the stag's ankle. Trey's rush was checked but he still caught Badger a blow, pitching him into the water. Plucky danced away, out of reach of the massive antlers, and ran round the other side of the Pond. He called to Badger who was swimming towards him.

'Here, Badger! There's an old empty sett nearby. Follow me!' He waited as long as he dared, then darted away as Trey rushed in pursuit. Badger reached the far side of the Pond and pulled himself on to dry land. He saw Plucky's escape route and rushed after him, just reaching the safety of the sett entrance as Trey galloped up.

'You're a brave one,' he said to Plucky. 'Once it's dark you must fetch the elders. Fox and Vixen and my other friends too.' The old creature gasped for breath. 'Tell them,' he panted, 'Badger's finished.'

CHAPTER EIGHT

Plucky stayed with Badger throughout the day, not daring to move. Trey eventually left the scene, with many bellowed threats about getting even. Plucky didn't stir until it grew dark. Badger had scarcely spoken all day, except in reply to questions about his comfort. He was in pain and very weak, but he willed himself to hold on for his friends. They must be told about the stream.

Plucky quickly made sure the area was safe and then ran straight for Fox and Vixen's earth. He lost no time in explaining Badger's plight.

'We must go to him at once,' Fox said. 'We won't wait for the others. Plucky, you must round them up. Now, where is the sett?'

Fox and Vixen ran off, hoping desperately to be in time. They were pleased to find Toad waiting for them.

'I've seen Badger,' he told them. 'I got the news from the frogs. He's in a bad way.' He led them to Badger's hideaway.

'Is he badly injured?' Vixen whispered.

'I don't think so. He's concerned mostly about

the stream,' Toad answered. 'He begged me not to go there.'

The three friends entered the sett. Badger gasped, 'Fox! Vixen! Thank goodness you're here.'

'Badger, my dear old friend,' Fox cried in distress. 'Whatever happened to you?'

'I'm done for. The stream's poisoned somehow and I drank from it. None of you must go near it. You must promise me!' he cried.

'Of course we promise,' Fox replied at once. 'But how do you know all this?'

Badger explained about the rabbit and what had happened to it and how he himself had already drunk the water before he knew of the real danger. 'Where are the others?' he demanded suddenly. 'Mole and Weasel and Adder. They must *all* promise.'

'On their way, all of them,' Fox assured him. 'Plucky will see to it.'

Badger quietened but the difficulty he was having breathing alarmed his friends.

'Oh Badger, is there nothing we can do for you?' Vixen wailed.

'Nothing,' the old creature answered. 'Don't worry, it's all my own fault. I'm old and I can accept whatever comes.' He fell into a doze. His friends stayed by his side, hardly speaking. Later a worried-looking Weasel joined them.

'Mossy's in a terrible state,' she told them. 'He and Badger you know, so close . . . But the journey here is too far for him. Friendly and Charmer are coming.'

Daylight returned though the sett, of course, remained in darkness. Badger's breathing had eased a little. He awoke to find the two younger foxes had arrived. 'Is everyone here?' he murmured. 'I don't see Mole or Adder.' (He still insisted on calling Mossy 'Mole', confusing him with the old Mole, his father.)

Weasel said, 'It's a long crawl for Adder, Badger. And it's dangerous for her in the light. You'll have to be patient.'

'Yes, yes, that crazed stag has sworn revenge on us all. I don't want any accidents on my account,' Badger nodded. 'Perhaps Mole should steer clear after all.'

'Quite right,' Fox spoke up. 'And he's doing just that.'

There was a commotion outside and Leveret tumbled into the sett under the nose of Trey. 'He's got us bottled up here all right,' he panted. 'He's patrolling outside just waiting for a false move.'

'He'll have a long wait then,' Friendly remarked grimly.

Angry snorts and stamps were clearly to be heard.

'This is absurd,' Fox said. 'Why ever should an animal bear such a grudge?'

'So far we've got the better of him,' Badger said. 'His pride's wounded. And so is his hide!' He almost laughed. 'He's got the scars to prove it.'

'Scars?' Fox echoed.

'Yes, Plucky and myself left our teeth-marks on him.'

'Did you though?' Fox was most impressed. 'Badger, you're not finished yet. Not by half.'

It was late in the day when Adder, travelling cautiously, arrived near the Pond. Not known for showing great concern for any of the other animals, she had come anyway. Badger was special and Adder wanted to see him for herself. She lay hidden amongst the pond-side plants, watching the stag pacing up and down. She also saw Whistler the heron searching the area.

Whistler's sharp eyes spied the snake. He landed awkwardly beside her.

'What are you doing?' the snake hissed. 'The stag will see us!'

'Urgent message,' the heron croaked. '*I* can't get into Badger's sett but you can. Pass the word on.'

'*What* word?' Adder rasped.

'The humans,' Whistler said. 'They've poisoned the stream. They've dumped – Whoops!' He interrupted himself and took to the air. Trey was running to investigate. 'I'll be back!' Whistler called.

Adder crossly buried herself in some dead leaves. Trey found nothing but, as soon as the stag had wandered away, Adder decided to make a break for cover. She didn't want Whistler endangering her again. Despite the heron's agitated cries of 'Wait! I didn't finish! It's important!' she ignored him totally and didn't stop wriggling until safe inside the sett.

Weasel came to look. 'Adder! What was the fuss about?'

'That stupid bird,' Adder muttered. 'Nearly got me caught.' She paused. 'How's Badger?'

'Hanging on. He's made all of us swear to avoid the stream.'

Adder was glad to go through this ritual promise. 'I thought I might not see you again,' she said. 'Is the pain very bad?'

'No worse,' Badger replied. 'But I'm so parched. I feel as if I could drink the Pond dry. And I haven't eaten for ages either.'

There were murmurs from his friends. 'What? You have an appetite?' Adder hissed.

'I think so – yes,' Badger admitted.

'Are you telling me I've slid right across this Park just to hear you complain you're hungry?'

'I – I can't help it,' Badger mumbled. 'It's only natural.'

'No, it isn't,' Adder hissed. 'Not for an animal who is supposed to be dying! And that's why I came. There's nothing wrong with you. You're an old humbug, Badger!'

'There *was* something wrong with me,' Badger insisted. 'But, I must say, I do begin to feel – '

'Better?' Weasel snapped. 'Then why all the bother?'

'Oh, Weasel! Now, Badger saw the rabbit die.

What was he to think?' Vixen said. 'If he's better we should all be celebrating, not complaining.'

The animals all began talking at once. Adder waited until it was quiet. 'Listen, everybody,' she lisped. 'Whistler has discovered something about the stream. He wants to tell us.'

Fox went to the exit to look for him. 'Whistler!' he called. 'Are you there?'

There was no answer. But Fox saw Trey was still at the pond-side. His anger kindled. 'Will he never give up?' he muttered. 'Why should we be holed up like this?' He ran back to the others. 'Badger, will you be all right now?'

'Yes, I think so, Fox. If I could get some food . . .'

'We'll bring you some,' Fox declared. 'We're not going to stay here! We all have to eat. Why are we letting this deer dictate to us?' He was thoroughly roused.

'Oh, this is more like the Farthing Wood Fox,' Friendly murmured to his sister.

'Come on, everyone. We ought to be able to deal with this beast after all we've been through,' Fox rallied them.

'Oh, what a joy to have such friends,' Badger remarked. 'If only Owl were here as well.'

'No good worrying about her,' Weasel said. 'She's out of reach.' She and the others followed Fox up the tunnel. Toad and Adder brought up the rear. The first animal they saw was not Trey, but Plucky, sitting calmly all by himself.

'Is Badger – ' he began earnestly.

'Blossoming,' Adder drawled. 'He simply adores all the attention.'

Plucky listened as Fox explained Badger's recovery.

'Wonderful news,' Plucky said. 'And now I've some for you. I've persuaded Trey to quit.'

'What? How could you do that?' Fox cried.

'Oh, I told him the other stags were making use of his absence and were becoming very friendly with the hinds. You should have seen him run!'

'Well!' exclaimed Vixen.

Friendly said, 'Plucky, you're a chip off the old block.'

Badger had been lucky and he knew it. 'If I hadn't seen that rabbit I'd be dead now,' he muttered to himself. He tottered to the mouth of the sett, unable to ignore his great thirst any longer. He tumbled head–first into the Pond and drank greedily. Later Fox and Vixen brought him food.

'Badger – the great survivor,' Fox joked happily.

After this Fox sought out Whistler.

'I've found a clue to the poison in the stream,' the heron announced. 'Outside the Park, where a ditch runs into the stream, humans have left some rubbish. It seems to me that that's where the poison is probably seeping into the water.'

'Yes. They poisoned the Great Stag and now we have Trey in his place,' Fox commented sourly.

'Not only the stag,' Whistler pointed out. 'There are no fish in the stream. I have to fly far afield to hunt. And dozens of small animals have died by the stream.'

Fox shuddered. 'All because of the humans' carelessness,' he said. 'Will they never learn?'

The time of the rut was approaching for the deer. Trey was fully occupied guarding his hinds against any would-be rivals, few as they were. So Badger returned safely to his old home to the delight of Mossy, his neighbour, and all the animals enjoyed a breathing space. Soon the roars and bellows of the stags shook the Park. Those bold enough to answer Trey's challenge soon discovered just how invincible he was. His strength overwhelmed them, and he chased them far from the females. His mastery was confirmed. He was a royal stag.

The mists of early autumn came in the evening to shroud the Park. Trey paced his domain in lordly fashion. White Deer Park was his kingdom and the inhabitants his subjects. But Nature had a lesson to teach him about the real meaning of dominion.

CHAPTER NINE

Owl was trapped in Farthinghurst, unable to stir from the Great Beech. Encased in the awful cement, her only possible movement was an awkward shuffle along the branch she used as a perch. Her one blessing was Hollow, the faithful male owl who kept her supplied with food.

Owl had given up all hope of returning to White Deer Park. She had found her mate; yet here she was, far from home, unable to show Hollow off to her friends. 'Why bother to bring food for me?' she hooted to Hollow miserably. 'I might as well starve and get it over with.'

Hollow tried to cheer her up. 'Things can only get better,' he said.

But as autumn arrived things only seemed to get worse. Rain poured down never-endingly, soaking the ground and making everything stream with water. The leaves on the beech dripped continuously on to Owl who had no shelter. One night Hollow shuffled restlessly on the branch.

'What's the matter with you?' Owl asked irritably.

'I feel worried. There's something . . . something is going to happen,' he replied uncertainly.

And there were other birds too who felt the same. Songbirds and starlings and such like, normally on their roosts at night, went wheeling and flitting about from one spot to another. Then a breeze began to blow which soon became a gale. But it didn't stop there. The beech rocked and shuddered as the wind grew even stronger. The noise of it was terrifying – a constant wailing howl which rose to a kind of scream as the wind's power tore at the landscape. It had become a hurricane.

The human population of Farthinghurst awoke in the dark as their homes shook and rattled. Chimneys toppled, power lines fell, glass shattered, sheds and outhouses were sent crashing like packs of cards. Pieces of fence, tiles, guttering were flung through the air like scraps of paper.

In the early hours of the morning the storm reached its height. The Great Beech stood alone and so bore the full brunt of the storm's power. The tree roots had been loosened by days of rain and, suddenly, these lost their grip. The great tree swayed and shifted. Hollow left his perch in terror and was tossed like a speck into a hedge where dozens of small birds were already cowering. Owl waited for the end.

With a last long sigh the beech toppled, its roots torn from the earth. It fell with a tremendous crash on to the soil that had nourished it for so long. Owl was hurled to the ground, the force of the wind blowing her clear of the beech on to softer ground. The breath was driven from her lungs, but the brittle cement that had trapped her wings and talons was smashed into pieces. She was free! Bruised and gasping, she stirred, flapping her aching wing muscles. She scurried for shelter and was flung into a small tree.

Towards daylight the hurricane passed, leaving a trail of destruction. There was damage everywhere. The surrounding countryside was changed for ever. And with the fall of the Great Beech, Farthing Wood now lived only in the memories of those who had known it.

Owl's first thought was for her friends in White Deer Park. How had they fared during the great storm? Now she could fly again, she was eager to begin her journey home. Her second thought was for Hollow. Had he managed to find shelter? She pulled herself out of the shrub. In a greyish light she saw the beech lying like a slaughtered giant where it had fallen. People were scurrying about, examining the damage to their houses. Owl took to the air, calling Hollow's name. He flew up to meet her, overjoyed to see her imprisonment was over.

'I have the storm to thank for that,' she told him. 'But now we must leave – we have a journey to make.'

Hollow followed willingly and they flew away

over Farthinghurst and its dazed human inhabitants. Owl led the way across the battered countryside. Everywhere there were changes – trees lying like skittles on the ground. Others still stood but had gaping wounds where great branches had been ripped from their trunks. Birds wheeled about, confused by the altered landscape, their roosts and nests destroyed. Owl wondered how much White Deer Park would be altered – and how many of her friends survived.

The two birds flew on without speaking, Owl navigating as best she could. At last, tiring, she called, 'Look out for a spot to rest.'

Hollow spied a small tree thickly covered with ivy, which looked suitable. 'Down there,' he said. 'Plenty of cover.'

They skimmed down. Owl could hardly wait for dusk. She was looking forward to being able to hunt for herself for the first time in ages. Despite her aching wing muscles, she was determined to be independent. So Hollow's next remark came as a shock.

'I'll carry on being the hunter,' he said. 'No need for you to bother.'

'But I – ' Owl began.

'No "buts",' Hollow interrupted. 'I can easily catch enough for both of us. You need plenty of rest. It's a wonder a bird of your age has come through such an experience at all.'

Owl felt insulted. 'I'm not *that* old,' she snapped.

'Yes, of course I'm tired. But my hunting days are not over by any means.'

'Don't *worry*,' Hollow replied. 'You needn't explain. I know you didn't take kindly to being fussed over when you couldn't fly. But, you see, I don't mind at all. I'm younger and fitter and I can do all that you used to do.'

Used to do! Owl looked insulted. Just let him wait! She'd show him. But she held her tongue for the moment. They both needed sleep.

Later, while Hollow was away on his search for prey, Owl left the ivy to do her own hunting. Her flight muscles were painfully stiff but she ignored the discomfort. 'I'm not going to be dependent any longer,' she vowed. 'At least my eyes are as good as ever.' But as she flew awkwardly over the fields she realized she would never be quick enough to pounce on the voles and mice she saw below. Her wing-beats grew slower and more laboured with each minute and she lost height. But she had one piece of luck. There was a mouse particularly careless of hunters, who was completely absorbed with his meal. Owl dropped down and grasped it. She had made a kill! She was proud and delighted, but all too soon she discovered she couldn't get airborne again. She simply couldn't beat her wings fast enough and she was stuck on the ground. Now, more than ever, she needed Hollow.

When the male owl finally arrived, Owl was awfully hungry. She had left the mouse to show her skill off to Hollow, but the other owl was contemptuous.

'What did I say to you, you silly old bird? I've been searching for you everywhere. I've caught enough to feed a whole family, let alone the two of us.' He landed and saw the mouse. 'And is this all you wore yourself out for? Someone else's leavings?'

'No, no, I caught this. I caught it!' Owl protested.

But Hollow wasn't listening. He was already taking off to fetch some of the food. 'You'd better eat heartily, you need to build your strength up,' he told her. 'And in future you ought to pay more attention to what I say. You've made a real fool of yourself! I shall have to watch you all the time, I can see.'

Owl groaned. She seemed to have made herself more dependent than ever.

CHAPTER TEN

In White Deer Park Trey's dominance had been accepted by the entire deer herd, males and females alike. The other stags kept their distance as Trey led the hinds to the Pond to drink. The Farthing Wood animals, who certainly hadn't accepted his dominance, watched as the deer bent to drink. Trey kept guard meanwhile over what he regarded as the herd's exclusive water supply.

Fox was angry. 'The Pond used to be our water-hole as well. Everyone had free use of it.'

'There's plenty of rainwater lying around,' Adder hissed 'Does it really matter?'

'The Pond is symbolic,' Weasel told her.

'Of what?'

'The way our freedom has been taken away by this stag.'

Adder looked bored but Weasel went on, 'There was a time, not so long ago, when we did more than just talk about such things.'

'We were younger then,' said Fox.

'We're still the Animals of Farthing Wood,' Weasel

reminded him. 'We've got the better of many a foe in our time.'

'We don't want to meddle with Trey,' Vixen warned. 'He's young, big and strong and all our cunning and experience may be no match for him.'

'I don't want to meddle with him,' Weasel retorted. 'I simply feel we should stand up for ourselves.'

'Bravo, Weasel,' said Friendly. 'Father, why don't you lead our party to the Pond to drink, just as Trey has done with his herd?'

'It'll only provoke him,' said Charmer, Friendly's sister.

Friendly looked at Fox. 'Well, Father?'

'All right,' he replied. 'We'll try it. He can't deal with a whole group of us.' He grinned. 'Well, no time like the present, eh? I feel younger already. Who's coming?'

There were many cries of support.

'Good,' Fox said. 'But Badger must stay behind. Mossy, you keep him company. Make sure he doesn't leave his sett.'

The animals gathered. Leveret joined the foxes and Weasel and Whistler. Adder showed no sign of wishing to be part of it. Mossy hastened to Badger's sett.

The old creature took the news badly. 'Oh, so they think I can't be of help any more?' he mumbled. 'How could Fox be so unkind?'

51

'He means to be the opposite,' Mossy assured him. 'He wants to protect you.'

'Protect me? That's not necessary. I can look after myself!' he declared and began to lumber up the tunnel.

'No, don't go,' Mossy called. 'Fox asked me to – '

'Keep me out of it?' Badger snapped. 'Oh no. *That'll* be the day. Where the Farthing Wood animals go, *I* go!' He left his sett and Mossy was powerless to stop him.

Adder was coiled up in the Hollow. As Badger passed the spot he questioned the snake. 'What are you doing here at such a time?'

Adder drawled, 'Being more sensible than you, Badger, I should guess.'

'Adder, we're all together in this. Have you forgotten the Oath?'

'Of course not. But whatever happens at the Pond will happen before *I* could get there.'

Badger realized this was probably true of himself, too. 'Very well, I'll see you later.'

'I hope so. Go carefully, Badger. There's something in the air tonight.'

The other animals had approached the Pond. Fox looked up and down its length. 'We have to be clever about this. We'll do our best to fox the stag.' His friends and relations enjoyed the pun.

'How do we do it?' Whistler asked.

'By doing what he least expects. We'll confront him!'

There were appreciative noises of support as Fox led them to the water under Trey's very nose. The stag's massive head swung round. 'What's this?' he bellowed.

'It's a drinking party,' Fox answered quietly and he and Vixen, followed by the rest, calmly passed him by. For some moments Trey stood motionless. Fox's bluff seemed to work. As the animals reached the water's edge Fox whispered, 'Get in amongst the hinds.'

His friends responded by pushing themselves between the bulky bodies of the deer as they drank. The sheer cheek of it roused Trey and he dashed forward. But the Farthing Wood animals were so mixed up among the female deer that Trey couldn't attack any of them. He snorted furiously and galloped up and down, looking vainly for an opening.

The hinds didn't mind the smaller animals being there. They had no fear of them and knew many of the older ones well. Fox in particular was held in high regard. Trey was the only member of the herd who had any ill-feeling towards the Farthing Wood band. The hinds actually began to chatter to them in a friendly way. From a spot amongst the reeds Toad chuckled, 'Good old Fox. He's left the stag helpless.'

Trey's fury was overwhelming. 'Stop your

prattling,' he roared at his females. 'Step away!' He knew Fox was making a fool of him.

The hinds turned to look. Trey pranced about, beside himself with rage. But nothing would have made them put Fox and Vixen in danger.

'Step away, I say,' the stag fumed, 'or you'll regret it!' His threats were idle. He couldn't harm his own herd.

A wind blew across the Park – a wind of ill-omen. All the creatures, save one, were aware of it and they paused, raising their heads and sniffing the air anxiously. Only Trey was oblivious, wrapped in his own importance as usual.

'We need shelter,' said Vixen. 'There's a storm brewing.' Even as she spoke the wind began to moan in the tree-tops and send wide ripples chasing across the Pond's surface.

Fox quickly began to round up his group. The hinds milled about nervously. 'Remember the place where Badger went when he thought he was dying?' Fox asked his friends. 'We must all go there now. No time to get back to our own homes.'

Plucky knew the way better than anyone. He trotted off, calling, 'Follow me.'

Trey saw his opportunity. 'You've taken one too many chances,' he growled savagely and lowered his antlers as he charged.

'Plucky! Plucky! Take care!' Vixen cried. She was just in time.

The young fox sidestepped the stag's hasty rush

which carried the great beast many metres onward. Fox scoffed, 'The mighty stag! He doesn't even pay any attention to the danger his own herd is in.'

Now the wind began to howl. Strong gusts whipped at the sedges and rushes by the Pond. Whistler flew up, croaking a warning. Trey's anger cooled as he watched the jittery behaviour of the hinds. They were fretful, not knowing what to do.

Fox turned and led the animals after Plucky. One by one they entered the deserted sett, gaining comfort from each other's company. Whistler joined Toad amongst the reeds.

'No contest,' Toad remarked. 'The Pond's ours again.' They watched Trey gathering the hinds. Then the deer moved away.

'They'd be wise to stay away from the trees,' Whistler remarked thoughtfully.

The strength of the wind grew with every passing minute. In a patch of woodland not far away Badger tried to hurry himself. He'd travelled too far from his own sett to be able to return in safety. He could think only of the haven where his friends, unknown to him, were now sheltering. He was between the two setts and he knew he was in great peril.

CHAPTER ELEVEN

In the teeth of the wind the deer herd stood on the open grassland. The other stags tried to join them, feeling exposed. Trey wouldn't allow them too close to the hinds. The hurricane reached its height. All the deer lay down, bunching instinctively. They listened to the crack of shattering branches, then the crashes of falling trees. The screaming wind seemed to laugh at the havoc it caused.

In the abandoned sett the Farthing Wood animals huddled together. Fox said to Vixen, 'I'm so glad Badger is safe in his own home.'

As he said it, in that other part of the Park Mossy dug himself deeper down into the ground as the tempest raged. He was frightened for Badger who hadn't returned. He feared the worst. Deeper and deeper went the little mole. Suddenly the entire system of underground tunnels and passages shook under the most tremendous blow. Mossy paused, trembling. One of the large trees had fallen directly on to Badger's sett, smashing through into the heart of his living quarters. So Badger, without being aware of it, had saved himself by ignoring Fox's advice. But he was still in awful danger.

With every stumbling step across the Park, Badger risked his own death. Branches and boughs fell all around him. As he scuttled free from one spot, another branch would snap and bar his way. Whole trees fell too and he knew somehow he must get into the open. 'It looks as though I escaped being poisoned only to be flattened by an oak,' he muttered grimly. He struggled on. Miraculously he at last saw light ahead; he was near the edge of the woodland. Exhausted, terrified and utterly breathless, he forced himself on to reach safety and then collapsed helplessly. At that moment the worst of the storm passed.

When the wind's force had slackened Trey scrambled to his feet. Nearby was a crumpled piece of fencing which once had marked the boundary of the Nature Reserve. Next to it a hefty Scots Pine, almost ripped from the earth, leant at a crazy angle. It swayed threateningly with every gust of air. Trey looked around at the other stags, some of whom were mingling within the herd. These got to their feet, watching Trey uncertainly.

'The danger is gone,' he boomed. 'Get away from my hinds.'

The males wandered a little way away but the dominant stag wasn't satisfied. '*All* the way – over there, through that gap! I want no rivals.' He followed up his words by cantering towards them.

Some of the males ran through the gap in the fence. The bolder ones refused to be driven out. Trey began to single them out, targeting them one by one for a final charge. Most of them scattered and he scented victory. But one large male stood his ground. Trey gave chase. The two animals went round and round, as the herd watched. The smaller of the two stags stumbled over the broken fencing and went sprawling, smashing against the pine tree which rocked to and fro. The tree teetered for a moment and, as Trey rushed forward beneath it, it crashed down on top of him, pinning him beneath its weight. The mighty royal stag lay motionless. The other male regained his feet. Then the entire herd gathered around Trey, looking in horror at his stricken body. He looked back helplessly through glassy eyes. Blood flowed from his open mouth.

Dawn broke over the shattered Park. Many trees had fallen. Many lives had been lost. In the Hollow, Adder uncoiled herself and slid away. During the fury of the hurricane she hadn't stirred a fraction.

It was a while before the Farthing Wood animals felt it was safe for them to leave the sett. It was daylight when Friendly went up the exit tunnel to look out.

'It's changed,' he whispered. 'Everything's changed.'

Around the Pond rushes and sedges were flattened. At one end a birch tree had crashed into the water and, farther away, a wooded area had been thinned out by the storm's savagery. The rest of the animals crowded round to look. The older ones were reminded of their past.

'It's like Farthing Wood when the bulldozers came,' Fox said sadly.

'But there *are* many trees left standing,' Weasel remarked optimistically. 'Or – or – leaning . . .'

'Yes, we must avoid the leaning trees,' Fox said at once. 'Listen! Hear them creaking . . .'

'What of your homes under the trees?' Leveret asked. 'Most of you live amongst woodland.'

'We must go and see if we need to make new ones,' Vixen said.

Toad came crawling from his shelter to greet them. 'What a night,' he croaked. 'Whistler's gone to inspect his nest.' He scanned the faces. 'But where's Badger?'

'Safe enough inside his own sett,' Friendly replied.

The animals wanted to get home quickly now. 'Remember,' Fox warned them. 'Tread carefully and avoid the leaning trees.'

Toad remained by the Pond. Fox and Vixen came across Badger who, in the lull, had revived and was continuing his journey. They were delighted to see each other and Badger explained what had happened to him.

'Foolish, loyal creature,' Fox murmured warmly. He described how Trey had been bested.

'You're heading home?' Badger asked. 'Then I'll go with you.'

All the way the three of them noticed the changed appearance of the Reserve. At one point they spotted the Warden inspecting the damage.

'He'll make it all right again,' Badger said confidently.

'It'll never be quite the same,' Fox remarked.

'We'll get used to the changes,' Vixen comforted him.

Whistler was flying to meet them. He had seen Trey's body from the air and hurried to spread the news. 'Quite astonishing,' he told them at once. 'For the second time this season a supreme stag has met his end. Trey is lying crushed by a tree.'

'Is he dead?'

'Dying.'

'And the rest of the herd?'

'No other casualties, I think.'

The animals had mixed feelings. It was fateful news for all of them.

'Forgive us,' Vixen said at last. 'We haven't even asked about your nest.'

'Wrecked,' Whistler answered. 'But nests are easy to replace. Unlike trees.' He left them and the three animals were reminded of what might lie ahead of them.

The foxes soon found they were lucky. Their earth was situated in a copse of young trees whose flexible trunks and branches had withstood the hurricane better than many of the rigid older ones.

'May you have the same luck, Badger,' Fox said.

The old creature trundled on to the nearby beech woodland where he had dug his sett. Here he found many well-grown trees had been uprooted. He travelled on a little farther and then stopped dead, staring at the crater in the ground which was all that remained of his home. It had been smashed beneath the tremendous impact of the fallen tree.

'My home,' he whispered. 'I have no home.' Over and over again he repeated the words. All at once the realization came to him of his narrow escape. There was no doubt he would have been killed had he stayed where Fox had wanted him to. Homeless he might be, but fortunate too. He gazed at the crushed sett, wondering how or where he would be able to construct a new one. He suddenly remembered Mossy.

'Oh! Mole! Where are you?' he wailed. 'Are you under all this?'

Mossy had been waiting not far away, keeping a look-out for his aged friend. He heard his voice and struggled towards him through the debris.

'Badger! You're safe! Thank goodness you didn't listen to me. Your stubbornness saved you.'

'It did indeed,' Badger admitted. 'And your home – is it intact?'

'Pretty well. Poor Badger, where will you live now?'

'I don't know,' the old animal answered. 'I'm a bit long in the tooth to be digging a new sett. But one thing – with the threat of Trey removed I could live . . . almost anywhere.'

Mossy was eager to hear about the stag and all their friends. Badger told him what he knew. Then he said, 'It seems I shall have to make one more journey – back to the abandoned sett. It's my best hope.'

'Won't you rest awhile before you go?' Mossy pleaded. 'You look so tired. I'll bring some worms for you.'

'Yes, yes, thank you, Mole. I'll just lie down here.'

Later that day Badger said farewell to Mossy and set off once again across the Park. He didn't hurry. There were a lot of obstacles in his path.

CHAPTER TWELVE

Badger, of course, was not the only creature made homeless by the storm. So when he finally reached the abandoned sett he found it already occupied. He smelt the smell of his own kind inside. Badger voices – young and not so young – could be heard. He sighed and went to the Pond to drink.

A young female badger was there. 'What a terrible storm,' she remarked. 'I've moved my family here. We lost our old place.'

'Yes. I'm homeless too,' the old animal muttered.

'Oh, how sad. But wait – there's plenty of room in this sett. You could share with us. We wouldn't interfere.'

'No, no,' Badger refused. 'You're very kind. But I'm not used to sharing. I'll find something, I'm sure.' He wandered away.

There didn't seem to be anything else suitable, however, wherever Badger looked. 'What a way to end up,' he murmured forlornly as he looked in vain for shelter. 'No home now, not anywhere.' He got so upset he became confused. Without realizing it he stumbled through one of the gaps in the broken fencing and out into open country. He continued to search blindly for a hole, a burrow, anything he could shelter in. Eventually, overcome by weariness, he lay down and fell asleep where he was.

When he awoke, he was still in a daze. He looked back at the Park. 'No use returning there,' he told himself. 'Only one home for me. My old home. In Farthing Wood.' His shock had scattered his wits. 'Now, let me see. Which way do I go?'

Back in the Nature Reserve, over the next few days, the inhabitants became used to seeing men around clearing away debris, mending fences, cutting down dangerous branches and trees. Trey's body had been removed by the Warden and, on his round of inspection, the man also discovered the poisonous containers that had been dumped near the stream. These were quickly disposed of, and the Warden began to make regular checks on the flowing water. Once it ran clean again, he would restock the stream with plants and animal life.

Whistler watched progress closely. 'When I see fish there again,' he told his friends, 'I'll know it's safe once more.'

No-one knew where Badger had gone. Fox and Vixen had seen his crushed home and Fox was quite sure the old fellow was no longer in the Park. 'He's wandered, I know,' he said brokenly. 'We've lost him, Vixen.'

Mossy sang out miserably, 'He couldn't find a home, he couldn't find a home.'

'First Owl and now Badger,' Fox moaned. 'What's happening to us? I can't bear it.'

'If Badger's outside the Park, why don't we go after him?' Weasel suggested.

'Which direction, pray?' Adder demanded. 'Are we all to risk losing ourselves?'

'You don't have to join in,' Weasel said. 'You should be underground in your winter sleep by now. Toad's already gone.'

'How can I sleep the winter away without knowing Badger's fate? I'll wait a little longer,' Adder decided. 'There have been no frosts yet.'

Whistler offered to fly out to look around now and again. 'Though I had no luck searching for Owl,' he added.

'Badger won't have gone far,' Friendly pointed out. 'He's on the ground.'

Badger meanwhile had paused to rest in the shadow of a large building. His wanderings had taken him as far as the church, the one recognizable feature in the immediate area. He remembered resting there before, with his friends, on their long journey. And as he snored in the open, his back pressed against the stonework, Owl and Hollow were heading for the very same building from the opposite direction.

The two owls had taken the journey at a comfortable

rate. Owl's wings were gradually becoming more supple. She had navigated very well and she told Hollow that when they reached the church they would be almost home.

They landed on the roof, Owl sensibly avoiding another encounter with the bats.

'So this is it at last,' Hollow breathed. 'I'll go hunting in White Deer Park tomorrow night!'

'Yes,' Owl said. 'And then you need not provide for me any more. I'll just – '

'Nonsense,' Hollow interrupted. 'No-one need know our arrangement. I shall carry on as before.' And he flew to bring Owl her supper for that night before she could protest further.

Owl heaved a sigh and watched the bats' darting flights. It was a clear night. Suddenly she spied the strikingly striped head of a badger below, lit by moonlight. She recognized her old friend at once.

'Badger! Badger!' she called, swooping down.

The old animal looked up, puzzled. 'Oh, Owl,' he said, 'you shouldn't have come looking for me.'

'I didn't come looking for you,' Owl replied. 'I've been away the whole of the summer. What on earth are you doing here?'

'I'm going home,' Badger mumbled.

'I should think so. But why have you left it?'

'Well, we all left it, didn't we, when we travelled across country to the . . . to the . . .'

Owl saw at once something was wrong. 'You're

not making sense,' she interrupted. 'Where are you heading?'

'Farthing Wood, of course.'

'FARTHING WOOD?!'

'Well, yes, I need shelter, I can't live out in the open.'

'Stop. Explain to me what's happened,' Owl asked Badger anxiously.

'I'm homeless, that's what's happened.'

Owl began to understand. She knew there must have been destruction in the Park and she dreaded what she would find. 'Where are the others?' she asked.

'Oh, *they're* all right,' Badger replied. 'They didn't lose their homes like me.'

Owl was relieved to hear the news. But she was moved by her old friend's plight. 'Now listen, dear Badger,' she said, 'there *is* no Farthing Wood. I've been back there and I can assure you there's not a stick left standing. What was once our Wood has been replaced by human dwellings.'

Badger tried to grasp this. 'You've been back there?' he asked.

'Yes.'

'Is that where you've been all this time?' Badger's wits seemed to be returning.

'Mostly.'

'But why did *you* go there?' Badger asked as a second owl approached them.

'Here's one reason,' Owl replied as Hollow

arrived, his beak crammed with food. 'Now, let's eat together.'

Gradually, as Owl described her adventures, Badger began to recover from his great shock. When they were ready, the three of them set off for the Park. Whistler saw the travellers, flew closer to make sure his eyes weren't deceiving him, and then with a croak of delight rushed to rouse Fox, Vixen, Weasel, and Adder.

They were all waiting as Badger found a gap in the fence and plodded through to the Park. The two owls accompanied him.

'I hardly dared hope for this,' Fox whispered as the friends all greeted each other joyfully.

'And, Owl, you've had company on your travels?' Vixen prompted.

Owl introduced Hollow proudly. 'I've a long tale to tell you,' she said. 'But that must wait for the moment.'

'Well, at least now I can hibernate,' Adder lisped. 'I've seen what I wanted to see and I bid you all farewell. Till the spring!'

As the snake slithered away Fox said, 'Come, Badger, we have something to show you.' He led the way. Close to Fox and Vixen's earth there were new diggings. Clods of soil were being thrown up as they watched.

'It's not quite ready yet,' Fox explained. 'But there

68

are many busy paws down there. You won't have long to wait.'

'Is it for me?' Badger gasped as Mossy emerged from the new sett with some younger foxes.

'Of course it's for you,' Fox answered as mole and badger were reunited. 'You're to be our near neighbour and we'll stay close together for the rest of our lives.'

'I think,' said Owl to Hollow, 'we can leave them to it for the present. I want to remind myself of my hunting terrain. Come on, I'll show you around.'

Hollow followed as she flew upwards. 'Well!' exclaimed Weasel. 'That's something I *never* thought I'd see.'

Part II

BATTLE FOR THE PARK

CHAPTER ONE

The winter that followed treated the animals of White Deer Park kindly. In the spring their numbers multiplied. Everything seemed settled and for the young animals there was time for play.

Plucky the young fox and Dash the yearling hare were firm friends. They had grown up together. More than anything Dash loved to run. One sunny day in April, as they gambolled about Dash challenged Plucky. 'Race me,' she said, 'as far as the leaning pine.'

'I never go near leaning trees,' Plucky answered. 'After the storm I'm very wary. Now, see that gorse bush?'

'Yes. Race you there and back again?'

'All right.'

Dash leapt off over the short spring grass. Plucky was soon left far behind. At the end of the race he was utterly breathless. Dash skipped about him. 'Have I exhausted you?' she asked.

'No, but I think we'll give up these races. They're too one-sided,' Plucky panted. 'You're such a wonderful runner!'

Dash looked pleased. 'If I could run over the downland like my father did,' she told him, 'then I'd *really* show you something.'

'Your father? When did he run over the downland?' Plucky asked.

'On the journey to White Deer Park, of course. With the other elders. When he was a leveret.'

Plucky nodded. 'And we still call him by that name. Well,' he continued, 'I don't think you'll ever have the chance. The Park fences have been strengthened since the hurricane. There's no way out.'

'It's not fair,' Dash complained. 'The birds aren't cooped up like we are.'

'We're not cooped up, Dash,' Plucky said firmly. 'We're protected here. And if you're so keen on racing, why don't you challenge one of the deer?'

'That's a great idea,' she answered and prepared to bound away.

'Don't go that way!' Plucky cried.

'Why not?'

'There are men approaching. Look!'

Although people had been appearing around the Reserve for some months now, the animals still kept away from them. Only the Warden was completely trusted. The visitors were carrying out a tally of all the Park's wildlife. After two mild winters numbers had increased so much that the Reserve was becoming crowded.

Plucky and Dash, like the rest of the animals,

knew nothing of this. The young fox led his companion towards the Pond.

'I bet Toad's around here somewhere,' Plucky remarked. He was fond of the smallest member of the Farthing Wood elders. Dash, however, wasn't so interested. As Plucky began to search, she ran off to find the deer herd.

Toad was paddling in the shallows beneath a fringe of rushes. He was an old toad and didn't exert himself too much. He was watching the mass of tadpoles that had hatched that spring. The Pond was alive with them. Plucky saw him and barked a greeting. Toad croaked an answer. Then he said, 'Where's your playmate?'

Plucky replied sadly, 'You know, Toad, sometimes she wears me out.' He noticed the tadpoles. 'Well, there's a feast for hungry fish!' he exclaimed. 'Oh, I'm sorry, some of them must be your – '

'Don't worry,' Toad interrupted cheerily. 'There are frogs' and toads' offspring in there. Can you tell the difference from here? *I* can't! And anyway, there are fewer fish in the pond now. The Warden's moved some to the stream.'

'The *stream*?' Plucky echoed. 'But does that mean the water's clean again?'

'Whistler thinks so. There are plants and all sorts of creatures in it now.'

Before Plucky could say any more there was a noise of galloping feet. They looked up. A young hind, running full-tilt, came into view. A blur of movement, which was Dash, streaked past her and then ran over to Plucky triumphantly.

'You see?' she cried, turning to look at the deer which had paused to drink. 'I'm unbeatable! There's nothing here to test me. I shall never know just how fast I am until I can get outside the Reserve and truly stretch my legs.'

'Don't be so silly,' Toad snapped. 'You can't go out of bounds. You'd be at risk.'

'Bah! Who could catch *me*?' Dash scoffed. 'Oh Plucky, won't you scrape a little exit for me under the fence somewhere? Just for me to use once to test myself?'

'Certainly not,' Plucky barked. 'I want you safe here.'

'Oh, you've no sense of adventure,' Dash complained. 'All right, I'll find someone else who can dig!' And with a look of scorn, she leapt away.

'She's a wilful young creature,' Toad commented. 'You'd better go after her, Plucky. Try to talk sense into her.'

'I'll try,' he replied. 'But I don't know if she'll listen.' He loped away, but Dash was soon out of sight and her trail was difficult to follow. Like all hares, she left a zigzagging track that sometimes doubled back on itself, and Plucky, unfortunately, lost it.

CHAPTER TWO

Badger's new home, close to Fox and Vixen's earth, was comfortable and suited him perfectly. Above all, he loved to be able to talk to his old friends whenever he wanted to. He and Fox were discussing how their little copse seemed much fuller of animals that spring when they saw Plucky approaching. He looked very worried.

'Have you seen Dash?' he asked at once.

'No,' the two elders answered together.

Plucky started to gabble out something about races and Dash's desire to stretch herself beyond the Reserve.

'Now calm down,' Fox advised. 'You can't do any more just now. You don't know where she is, so don't get worked up unnecessarily. Besides, I can't believe any creature here would be so foolish as to *help* her leave the Park.'

Plucky was comforted. Fox was so wise and experienced.

'As soon as Vixen or I see Dash,' Fox went on, 'we'll talk her out of these daft ideas. And I'm sure Badger feels the same.'

'Of course,' said Badger.

Later Fox told Vixen about it all. 'Poor Plucky was really alarmed,' he said. 'So I didn't mention what I really thought – that the rabbits can tunnel. And we both know how unpredictable *they* can be.'

Dash actually had forgotten her silly threat once she had got over her disappointment. She wouldn't have upset Plucky for the world. So she contented herself with tearing about the Park, from one side to the other, and racing any animal who would take up her challenge. This was all right for a while but as she always beat each creature with ease, she soon grew bored. Then she wanted Plucky's company again. So eventually she began to search for him.

She covered the entire Park except for one small area where the people had been working. And, strangely, now it was Dash who drew a blank. She appealed to her father who told her that, as Plucky was a fox, it would be more sensible to speak to the foxes.

'We don't see Plucky as often as you might think,' Vixen told the young hare. 'He has his own life to lead. But what's going on between you two? He was here asking about you a while ago.'

'Yes, I'd been behaving in a silly way,' Dash owned up. 'But that was only for a moment. This is different. Plucky is simply not around any more, Vixen. He's disappeared.'

'Have you looked everywhere?'

'Everywhere. I'm so afraid he's been injured somewhere and can't move.'

Vixen was reminded of how Trey had been crushed by a tree. She looked concerned.' There are still accidents,' she murmured, 'from time to time.'

'Plucky was always so careful,' Dash wailed. 'He wouldn't go near a leaning tree or anything unsafe.'

'Well, don't alarm yourself too much,' Vixen replied. 'We've plenty of friends to keep their eyes open for him. One of the birds is sure to spot him, if no-one else.'

'Owl won't be much use,' Dash muttered, 'Father says she's completely wrapped up with Hollow.'

'She'll rally round when we speak to her,' Vixen said. 'She always does. Now you mustn't fret. We'll have some better news for you soon.'

'Thank you, Vixen,' said Dash. 'You're such a comfort.'

Yet time passed and there was no better news. All the Farthing Wood friends had sought Plucky high and low without success. Dash, lonely and forlorn, could bear it no longer. She decided she would look outside the Park. The idea frightened her but she couldn't remove the nagging idea from her head that Plucky had taken her silly remark seriously and left the Reserve to search for her, in which case the two of them were going round and round looking for each other in a quite hopeless way.

'I'll persuade one of the rabbits to help me,' Dash told herself, just as Fox had feared. 'If Plucky has suffered because of me, I'll never forgive myself.'

CHAPTER THREE

Dash had to think up a story to persuade the rabbits to dig an exit for her. So she told a group of them she had a favourite food-plant just out of reach on the other side of the fence. The rabbits fell for it. They knew all about favourite plants. And so that was how Dash left the Park, her only home since birth, and found herself on the wide open downland.

In time the Farthing Wood animals became aware that not only Plucky, but now Dash was missing from the Reserve. And about the same time other creatures – squirrels, hedgehogs, rabbits – began to disappear. The elders were puzzled and alarmed. They gathered in their usual meeting-place.

'Odd that I should have remarked how crowded our copse was,' Badger said. 'Now it's quite the opposite.'

'It's happening all over the Park,' Leveret said.

'Wherever can they be going?' Weasel asked.

'We need to find out,' Adder lisped, 'before any more of us go missing.'

'The birds are our best hope,' Fox said. 'Owl, Whistler, perhaps you could scout around a bit?'

'I'm afraid I'd be of little use to you, Fox,' Whistler answered ruefully. 'I can't fly without discomfort. My old wonky wing is really playing me up.'

'Well, it's no use expecting me to do it,' Owl said haughtily. 'I have Hollow to think of now.'

'We're not getting very far,' Friendly remarked impatiently. He turned to Fox. 'Father, shall I see if I can pick up a clue somewhere?'

'Certainly. You know, I've a feeling humans are involved in this business.'

'Could it be anything to do with rats?' Toad asked idly.

'Rats?' the others cried. 'What rats?'

'The ones in the Park, of course,' replied Toad. 'Hasn't anyone else seen them?'

'Hollow and I have killed one or two,' Owl remarked.

'Well, they come to the Pond now and then to drink,' Toad resumed. 'And there are more entering the Reserve all the time.'

'Why haven't you said anything before?' Fox demanded.

'I thought you knew.'

'All right. Now I do know, let me warn you all. Rats are dangerous. They can spread disease. And they eat *anything*. Small creatures, eggs, young birds.

82

They're fierce and cunning. We must kill them whenever and wherever we find them!'

Fox's warning shook the Farthing Wood community. They realized that once again they had to band together to fight a common foe – to save their homes and themselves.

So far there weren't a lot of rats. Then, during a rainy spell, they were seen in ones or twos all over the Park. They climbed the fences or dug underneath them. Their homes outside the Reserve had been flooded in the downpours and they were looking for more secure sites. White Deer Park, where the human enemy was rarely seen, was like a magnet to them. Soon all the residents of the Reserve realized that they had a battle to face.

Weasel was the next to disappear. Her friends, busy with their rat hunting, didn't miss her at first. But, as they met together in little groups, they came to realize Weasel was no longer among them. They wondered which of them would vanish next.

Out on the downland Dash had come to no harm. She had kept well away from prying human eyes as she sought her playmate. After a while she knew she must give up her search. There was no clue anywhere to Plucky's disappearance. Sadly, early one morning, she ran back to the scrape under the boundary fence. This spot had been well used since she left the Park. The soil had been trampled. But Dash knew nothing of the invading rats.

She heaved a sigh of relief once inside White Deer Park again. She longed for news of Plucky and hastened towards Fox and Vixen's earth. She hadn't travelled far when she noticed a small group of men in her path. Something about their pose and their stillness alarmed her. She veered and doubled back, approaching the men from behind. She was curious despite herself. The men were strung out in a line, as if waiting for something. Dash hid herself behind a tall plant. A van was parked nearby on a flat piece of ground. From it muffled animal noises – anxious cries – reached Dash's sensitive ears. She saw a ripple of movement in one of the crates stowed inside the vehicle. Then another . . . and another. Animals were trapped inside them!

Dash was about to race away when she saw another creature captured. She also saw the cunning of the humans. She hadn't noticed – just as none of the captured animals had noticed – that there was a camouflaged net in front of the line of men, half obscured by shrubs and bushes. Other humans hidden elsewhere began to create a row, shouting and banging. An animal – a rabbit – was driven from cover in a panic. It blundered stupidly into the folds of the net, entangling itself. A man pounced and held it fast. Another came with a sack. The rabbit was bundled into it and then transferred to the van. Horrified, Dash watched two more small creatures taken before she made her escape. Here was the explanation for Plucky's disappearance, she felt sure. Were there bands of humans all over the Reserve doing the same thing? She pelted across the Park to the Farthing Wood animals' corner. She had to tell everyone to beware.

She burst into Fox and Badger's little wood, calling for Vixen. It was daylight and the foxes were sleeping. Vixen eventually appeared at her den's entrance, blinking sleepily. 'What is it?' she murmured. 'Dash! It's you! We'd given you up. We thought you were lost like the others.'

Dash gasped. 'The others?'

'Plucky and Weasel.'

'Weasel too? Oh, let me tell you, Vixen.' She panted out all she knew, explaining where she had been and what she had stumbled across on her return. 'It's the humans!' she cried at the end. 'The humans are taking the animals!'

Vixen, shocked, quickly roused Fox. He came at once, shaking himself awake. 'You say the animals are being trapped?' he barked. 'Under the Warden's nose? In a wildlife sanctuary?' He shook his head, his thoughts racing. 'There must be a reason for this. Perhaps it's for the animals' safety.' He spoke his thoughts aloud.

'How can anywhere be safer than here?' Vixen questioned.

Fox looked at her steadily. 'The rats,' he said

slowly. 'Maybe they're infecting other animals. The Warden would have to do something to protect us.'

'Wouldn't he first try to get rid of the rats?' Vixen asked.

Fox had to agree. 'Then what can it be?'

Dash begged the foxes to explain to her about the rats.

'Brown rats are invading the Park,' Fox told her. 'We've been trying to keep them in check.' He recalled the force of Dash's message. 'Where are these men?' he suddenly barked.

'Near the deer pasture,' she answered nervously, a little startled.

'I think we should go without delay, Vixen,' Fox continued. 'Dash can go with us. We have to find out where the animals are being taken. Plucky and Weasel must be rescued!'

CHAPTER FOUR

Fox and Vixen ran silently after Dash. Every so often the young hare paused to allow them to catch up. As they neared the place where the trap for the animals had been laid, they could see that the men had finished their task. They were packing up, bundling their equipment into the van along with the animals taken that morning. Two men then drove the van slowly away, taking care not to jolt the contents. The other men walked behind. Fox, Vixen and Dash watched them from a safe distance.

'Stay here,' Fox told the other two. 'I'm going to follow them.' Keeping well back, he tracked them to the Warden's cottage.

The Warden of White Deer Park came to meet the men, and proceeded to open the heavy park gate for the van to go through. Fox couldn't believe his eyes. Here was the protector of the Park wildlife permitting creatures to be whisked away! He slunk off, bewildered and sad. The Warden and the remaining men entered the cottage.

Dash was dancing about with impatience. 'Where did they go?' she shrilled as she saw Fox.

'Out of the Park,' Fox mumbled. 'I – I couldn't pursue them. I don't understand why – '

'I can follow them!' Dash interrupted. 'I'm fast! Which direction, Fox?'

Fox and Vixen began to protest about the dangers but Dash brushed them aside. '*Someone* has to find where our friends are being taken. And I'm the only one who can do it!'

Fox saw the sense and led her at a run to the open Park gate. Dash leapt away. Her speed soon brought her within sight of the van which was travelling slowly along the track leading to the nearby road. When it reached the road it speeded up. Here was a difficulty for Dash who couldn't run amongst traffic. She pulled up sharply, her heart pounding.

'Oh dear,' she cried. 'Now what do I do?' She looked around hurriedly. The downland stretched ahead of her, parallel to the road. 'That's my way!' she whooped in delight and raced on to the springy turf. Now at last the moment had arrived for her to test herself. Exerting every muscle, she flew over the grass. The van was visible below on the road. She kept more or less level until the vehicle slowed to turn into another track through the countryside.

'I didn't lose them, I didn't lose them,' she chortled to herself, thrilled with her efforts.

When it was safe she dropped down to this new track and watched the van approach a high wall. There was a double door in its centre. The van stopped. Its driver unlocked the doors and swung them wide. Dash was just close enough to see through to a vista of greenery – pasture and woodland very similar to White Deer Park itself. At last she knew where Plucky, Weasel and all the others had been taken.

It didn't take her long to retrace her journey. As she approached the Park the Warden's Land Rover swung into the drive. Dash skipped aside in the nick of time. She shot through the open gate and didn't stop running until she was well clear. The Warden stopped and closed the gate, then continued his journey to the walled park in which the van with its store of animals was now enclosed.

Fox and Vixen had returned to their home area where Badger, Friendly and Dash's father, Leveret, had joined them. Dash tumbled into their midst, tired, excited and bursting with her news.

Fox gasped, 'Did you succeed?'

'Yes, completely,' Dash cried. 'I've seen the place where the men take all the creatures. It's like another park! I can't make it out. If they're to be released *there*, why were they taken from here to begin with?'

No-one answered. They exchanged dumbfounded glances. Suddenly they all began talking at once, asking Dash to tell them exactly what this second 'park' was like.

She described it as best she could, laying great stress on the fact that a high wall surrounded it. 'I

don't think any animal could escape through that,'
she finished by saying.

'Then over it perhaps?' her father suggested.

'Far too high, Father.'

'Maybe under it?'

'It looks too solid. No gaps anywhere.'

'It's banishment then,' Friendly summed up. 'All
those animals are entirely in human hands.'

Fox looked fierce. 'We can't let this happen to
Plucky or Weasel,' he vowed.

'I'm always ready to help,' Badger responded. 'We
must rescue them, Fox. The Oath we all swore binds
us together still. There's no time to waste.'

'Dear Badger,' Vixen whispered.

Fox looked affectionately at the old creature, wag-
ging his tail. Even Badger's stout old heart couldn't
overcome his extreme age. 'You know, you'll be
most useful here,' he said. 'We need someone to
keep tabs on those rats.'

'Just as you wish,' Badger replied, not displeased.

'So – to the rescue group,' Fox resumed. 'We
need the assistance of the birds. One of us has to
get inside this new area to see the lie of the land
and, most importantly, to locate the animals themselves. Now Whistler's out of the question at
present.'

'That leaves Owl,' Friendly remarked doubtfully.

'Will she help?' Leveret asked.

'We can but ask,' said Fox. 'Hollow seems to take
all her attention, but her sense of loyalty is still there.'

90

'Leave her to me,' said Badger. 'I'll win her over. We're old companions and I think I know how to appeal to her.'

'Badger, you're a marvel,' Fox remarked wonderingly. 'You almost seem back to your old self.'

'Well, yes, Fox,' Badger answered. 'All I need is a sense of purpose.'

The round-ups continued. Animals in the Park were alarmed and spoke of nothing else. Fox racked his brains for an explanation for the Warden's involvement. He couldn't find one except that he was sure the man must somehow have a worthy motive. Meanwhile Plucky and Weasel were trapped.

True to his word, Badger sought out Owl. He found her with Hollow, her mate, feeding from their night's tally of rats. Badger complimented them on the number.

'Hunting's never been easier,' said Owl. 'One doesn't have to look far for prey these days.'

'Actually, your help, Owl,' said Badger, 'is needed in another way.'

Owl ruffled her feathers and resettled them. 'In what way?'

Badger explained about the walled enclosure and how only a bird could go over it.

'And that's to be me, is it?' Owl guessed. 'Well, of course,' she continued sarcastically, 'it would be Owl's job to stick her neck out.'

'There'd be no risk,' Badger assured her.

'Oh no. Only no-one knows exactly what's behind this wall. So if there are groups of humans around taking pot-shots at anything that moves and you don't see me return, you'll know the rest of you must avoid the place.'

'Oh really!' Badger exclaimed. 'Since when has the Warden used a gun on anything?'

'The Warden? Is he part of this?' Owl asked in surprise.

'We think he's organizing the transfer of the cap-tured beasts.'

'Oh, I see.'

'And, surely, Owl, you must agree we have to find where Weasel is and bring her back?'

'Ah, so I'm searching for Weasel, am I?' Owl exploded. 'Me, of all creatures! Oh yes, we're the greatest of friends, *we* are.'

'Now, Owl,' Badger reasoned gently, 'Weasel needs your help. Are you prepared to give it?'

She could give only one answer. 'If you put it that way, Badger, I'll – er – do all I can.' She looked awkwardly at Hollow.

'You told me you'd do no more adventuring,' Hollow reminded her crossly.

'It's not an adventure, Hollow, it's . . .'

'A rescue,' Badger finished for her. 'And there's Plucky to think about too.'

'I know all about your precious Oath,' Hollow remarked sourly, 'so she'll have to go, won't she?'

'Good,' Badger said. 'No-one is as clever as you, Owl, in the dark.'

She preened herself. 'When do we go?'

'Soon. Fox will decide. I won't be joining you, regrettably. There are things to concern us here too.'

Badger was right. Under cover of night more rats were arriving in the Park and making it their home. During daylight hours they kept out of sight, away from human eyes. Since some of the animals being rounded up were the very predators who could have kept the rats down, the rodents were able to spread quickly. They liked to be close to water. Toad and the frogs watched their growing numbers near the Pond with alarm.

Despite some losses, the rats' cunning and adaptability helped them to recover from any setback. They were able to eat almost anything. They were savage killers. They raided birds' nests, they were excellent climbers and swimmers. Not one area of the Park was left free from their intrusion. The Nature Reserve was the perfect place for them, away from their greatest enemy – people.

The Farthing Wood animals continued to hunt them, as did other creatures born and reared in the Park. But the invasion couldn't be stopped. Fox complained to his friends, 'How *can* the Warden be blind to what's happening here?'

'We can't wait for him to take action,' Badger told him. 'The man's attention is on the new Reserve.'

'The what?' Fox asked sharply. 'A new Reserve?'

'Yes, of course, the other enclosure,' Badger grunted. 'What else can it be? Animals must have been moved there to build up a stock in the place. The Warden has turned his back on us in favour of them. Perhaps the creatures taken there are really the fortunate ones. They at least are away from the rats' menace.'

'So we're to be left in the lurch?' Fox muttered bitterly. 'No, it doesn't make sense. This has always been a Nature Reserve. However, if we're to fight the rats alone, so be it. We need every tooth and claw, every beak and talon on our side. We will wage war and we will need all the support we can get from the predators taken to the new enclosure as well as those still here. So we have to gain entry to it.' He looked straight at Badger. 'I'm leaving you in charge here, old friend. Dash must lead us to the other Reserve tonight. You were quite right. We must take action ourselves at once.'

CHAPTER FIVE

It was a cloudy night and perfectly dark. The rescue group of Fox, Vixen, Friendly, Dash and Owl made their way to Dash's scrape. Owl perched on top of the fence as the animals squeezed through. Dash, eager and full of importance, led them without mishap to the high wall of the enclosure.

'Anyone behind that is well and truly sealed in,' Friendly commented.

'Owl, you're our only hope,' said Fox. 'See if there is a chink somewhere in this awful barrier.'

The bird alighted on the top of the wall. Her head swivelled as she scanned the strange park with her huge eyes. 'I suppose I must call for Weasel?' she fluted.

'Yes, try to find her,' Fox answered. 'Anything she can tell us about this place will be useful.'

Owl swooped over the unfamiliar parkland, calling every so often. She was surprised to discover just how similar the terrain was to that of White Deer Park, although it was far smaller. 'Almost a companion park,' she said to herself. 'And so it would

95

make sense, if one Reserve *is* overcrowded, to move animals to another one.' She continued to call, but Weasel didn't respond. 'Weasel! Weasel! Can you hear me? You *must* be able to!' She was becoming impatient. 'WEASEL!'

She rested in a pine tree. 'She's hiding from me,' she complained. Then she called her own owl sound, 'Ke-wick! Ke-wick!', a call familiar to all her old friends. This finally produced not Weasel, but Plucky, who came running.

'Owl? Is it you?' he barked excitedly.

Owl was relieved. 'At least *you're* not deaf,' was her comment.

'What are you doing here?'

'Looking for you, of course. And Weasel, who is ignoring me.'

'She can't hear you. She's part of the tunnelling party underground,' Plucky explained.

'Underground? Typical! Just when I'm calling her!'

'She wouldn't know that, would she?' Plucky reasoned.

'Hm. Well, I'm glad to see *you*, anyway, Plucky. Your relations, Fox, Vixen and Friendly – and a special friend of yours – have come on a rescue mission.'

'Special friend?' Plucky cried. 'You mean Dash? She's not lost then?'

'No, no. She discovered this place actually. It's another park, isn't it? What do you do here?'

'Try to think of ways of getting out, mainly,' Plucky answered. 'That's what Weasel and the others are up to. But it *is* a sort of park. Everything goes on as it does at home. Once we were released, we were left alone to live as before. Some creatures have accepted their lot. But others want to get back to their real dens and their families. I don't know why we had to be moved.'

'I have a theory about that,' Owl said. 'But never mind about that for the moment. Have you found a gap in the wall anywhere?'

'Not the tiniest crack,' Plucky replied bluntly. 'I don't think anything except a bird like yourself could get in or out without human say-so.'

'What about the tunnelling you mentioned?'

'No luck so far. Weasel, stoats and a young badger have been trying to dig underneath, but the wall goes down so deep. What we need here is an army of moles. Of course, the humans couldn't round any of *them* up.'

'Can you find Weasel? Just in case there's any new development.'

'Yes, I know where she is. Will you wait here?'

'I will. And be quick, Plucky.'

Weasel came soon enough. 'Well, I *am* honoured,' she quipped, 'that you should fly all this way for my benefit.'

'I didn't,' Owl corrected her at once, 'Don't flatter

yourself. I'm one of a party come to rescue you and others, too.'

'Where are the rest?'

'Waiting outside. Fox sent me in to find if there was – um – a loophole. Plucky says not. Have you discovered anything?'

'Only that there's no way out of here for a creature on four legs,' Weasel replied baldly. 'We've dug and dug and we can't reach the bottom. It might as well be solid rock. So we're all here to stay. And your rescue party will never get in here unless they get themselves captured first!'

'That would hardly help, would it?' Owl remarked pompously.

'I wasn't suggesting it, you silly – ' Weasel began, but Plucky cut in hastily.

'Please, we're supposed to be helping each other! Owl, can't you at least go and tell Fox and the others that you've found us and that we're unharmed?'

'Of course.' Owl glanced down at Weasel with a mite of sympathy. 'It doesn't do any good to fall out. I – er – I'm sorry, Weasel, for your difficulties. I'm sure you never asked to be brought here.'

Weasel was soothed. 'No, indeed. And thank you for your kind words. You're not a bad old bird really.'

'I'm glad you think so,' Owl replied. 'Take care of yourselves, both of you. We must think of another plan.' She flew away.

Dash and the foxes were in a fever of impatience.

They had waited for Owl a long time. At last she
appeared.

'It's hopeless,' she announced and explained why.
'Weasel and Plucky are safe, but they're also just
about as secure as the humans could make them.'

CHAPTER SIX

The rescue party had no choice but to return to White Deer Park. They were very disappointed. Dash, however, felt great relief at knowing at last where Plucky was.

'I'm going to get Weasel and Plucky out of there somehow,' Fox muttered with grim determination.

'Not you alone,' Vixen said. 'We all have our part to play, don't we, Owl?'

'Oh yes, of course,' she hooted in reply, though secretly hoping not to be troubled again. 'But that enclosure is not so bad, you know. The animals can live in it just as we do here. I believe the humans had their interests in mind when they moved them there.'

'You think like Badger then – that it's another Nature Reserve?' Fox queried. 'It does seem likely, doesn't it?'

'Yes,' said Owl, 'and so we in White Deer Park now have more space.'

'More space for us means more gaps for rats to fill,' Friendly reminded her sourly.

Despite the constant rat hunting, the rodents' numbers never seemed to drop. No matter how many the hunters slew, more took their place.

'There are too many of them and not enough of us,' Badger said. 'We need Weasel badly, and as many of her kind as we can get.'

The rats, of course, were not invisible and the time came when some of them fell foul of the human beaters and the line of nets. Once these were discovered, the other animals were no longer alone in their fight. They had allies, and powerful ones too. The rats knew this. And they knew that the humans would be on the warpath. So, as always, they tried to keep one step ahead,

At night the adult rats moved away from the Park, abandoning their burrows and settlements and returning to their old haunts in the local sewer system. Only nursing females remained in the Reserve because they couldn't travel. The rats were cunning. They planned to bide their time until the alarm was over, then go back to the Park and breathe country air again. One of the biggest males, a rat called Bully, vowed vengeance on the animals who had hunted them.

'We can't fight two enemies,' he snarled. 'A retreat was necessary. But the humans will forget us when they think they've driven us out. They have so many other plans buzzing in their great heads, don't they? Then we'll steal back, a few at a time, and build up our colonies once more. If you listen to me, all of you, and do as I say, we can take over the entire Reserve! We'll be so numerous we'll *flood* the rest of the creatures into submission. Are you with old Bully?'

There was a chorus of approval just as Bully knew there would be. He was a natural leader and the rat hordes needed direction.

'So be it,' he grunted. 'We're used to these smelly tunnels, we rather like them, don't we? But when we feel like a change next time, we'll have it. *Nothing* will stop us!'

The Farthing Wood animals were delighted with the rats' disappearance and guessed the humans were behind it. Now there was time to plan Weasel's and Plucky's return to the fold. Fox thought he might have the answer in Weasel's case; Plucky would be more difficult. He paid a visit to Whistler.

The heron was easy to find on the stream's bank. 'Glad to see you, Whistler,' Fox greeted him. 'How's the fishing? I believe you've lost weight?'

'I have. There's precious little to eat here. I did catch one fish, but it'll be a long while before stocks build up again.'

'Are you able to fly further afield?' Fox asked.

'I suppose so, but it taxes me rather.'

'You see, I have a favour to ask,' Fox explained.

'Speak on, Fox.'

'We know where Weasel is.' Fox described how Owl had found her and Plucky trapped in the enclosure. 'Now Weasel's a small creature,' he continued. 'Do you remember, on our journey to White Deer Park, how we all crossed the motorway?'

'Certainly,' Whistler replied. 'Oh, I understand you!' he cried. 'You're thinking of how I carried Weasel across the road?'

'Yes. Could you do it again? Just over the Park wall?'

'Well, I'm very creaky. I'd be willing to try, but I'd hate to drop her.'

'I'm sure you wouldn't do that. Perhaps you could practise a bit with a stick or two?'

'All right,' Whistler agreed. 'Although the main thing is to build up my strength.'

'I'll help you,' Fox offered. 'I can bring you some prey.'

The improvement in Whistler's diet raised his spirits a good deal. When he felt ready to tackle his mission, he took off for Fox's earth. He beat his wings with gritty determination, doing his best to ignore his aches and pains.

Fox had forewarned Owl she would be needed to show Whistler the way to the new park. When the heron was directed to her it was daylight, so Owl was asleep. Whistler called to her with his harsh cry.

'Is that you, Whistler?' Owl muttered sleepily.

103

'You might have allowed me a little more shut-eye. We're not all daytime flyers, you know.'

'Ah, there you are,' Whistler said, peering through the leaves of the beech tree where Owl was snoozing. 'I'm sorry to disturb you. I can wait a while if you prefer.'

'No point now I'm awake, is there?' Owl grumbled. 'The sooner I take you to the spot the sooner I can get back.' She shuffled forward and flapped abruptly into flight. Whistler followed her.

They reached the high wall. 'This is the place,' Owl told her companion. 'You'll find Weasel soon enough if you call.' She prepared to leave.

'Wait! Wait, old friend!' Whistler croaked.

'Now what?' Owl demanded irritably.

'Well, that's a large area in there. Can't you give me a clue as to where Weasel's likely to be? My wings do give me pain if I fly too far. I know you want to get back to your sleep, but please help a little.'

'Apologies, Whistler. Follow me. I'll try to pinpoint the spot where Plucky found me.' She flew straight to the very same pine tree as before. 'Now,' she said, 'you can call Plucky or Weasel. One of them's bound to come.' She took off at once.

'I can't carry Plucky out of here,' Whistler protested but Owl was already on the way home.

Whistler hadn't called for long when Plucky, once again, was the first to hear. The heron explained why he was there, stressing that of course he could only carry the very lightest of creatures. Plucky was excited by this idea and hurried to find Weasel.

'Well!' Weasel exclaimed when Plucky told her. 'This is marvellous news. I bet Fox is behind it, the clever old fellow. Lead on, Plucky.'

Whistler fluttered to the ground as he saw them coming. 'Here's your escape route, Weasel,' he joked.

'Not for the first time,' Weasel replied. 'I'm most grateful to you, Whistler. I've been itching to get back to my friends.'

Plucky looked glum. He knew he would have to remain.

'I'm so sorry,' Whistler said. 'I wish I could help you too.'

'Don't worry,' Plucky answered bravely. 'I'll get myself out, even if it means going out the same way I came in.'

Whistler and Weasel looked puzzled. Plucky merely said, 'Good luck, Weasel. And tell Dash when you see her, we'll soon be running together again in our own Park.'

Whistler turned to Weasel. 'Are you ready then?'

'I am.'

Whistler opened his beak and, very gently, grasped his friend until he had her in a firm grip. Then he took to the air, relieved to find Weasel was so light. Once over the enclosure wall Whistler found a soft spot for his landing. He released his passenger on to the springy turf.

'Any discomfort?' he asked.

'None at all, I thank you.'
'You know the way now?'
'I should think I do,' said Weasel.

CHAPTER SEVEN

Not long after Weasel's return she was able to pass Plucky's message on to Dash.

'I wish I could believe it,' she said sadly. 'But how can it be? He can't be airlifted out like you were.'

She moped around, thinking of how lonely he must be without any of his friends around him. Then all at once she realized there was something she could do. Plucky couldn't come to her, but she could go to him. She would get herself captured!

'There's no fun in White Deer Park anymore,' she told herself. 'I may as well go to the other place.' She set off excitedly to find the group of men with their nets, going straight to the area where she had first seen them. There was no-one there. She ran towards the Warden's cottage. All was quiet. By the time she had run all over the Park she realized the men had gone for good. The programme for reducing the over-population in the Reserve had obviously been completed. She lay down miserably in some long grass and, after a while, fell asleep.

Badger and Owl were right about the humans'

intentions. The other enclosure *had* been set aside for wildlife from the crowded Park. It had once been the walled grounds of a country house. The building had fallen into ruin and its land was bequeathed to the Country Naturalists' Trust. So eventually the White Deer Park Warden had become responsible for it. The enclosure had no name and there were no deer in it. The Warden was talking to another local landowner in the hope of further adding to it by the purchase of a neighbouring piece of land.

In White Deer Park itself the lull caused by the rats' retreat was about to end, for the rodents had achieved their purpose. The humans had been bamboozled, thinking their threat was over. And news that, once again, only one man walked the Reserve soon reached Bully and his sly comrades.

'Our patience has paid off,' he sneered. 'The Park is unguarded. But we won't make ourselves noticeable. Oh no, we know better. We'll creep back in little bunches. A few at a time is the way. And we'll spread across the Park in stages. No-one will suspect; we're only small, aren't we?'

So the rats returned, little by little, over many nights. They were quiet and careful and the Park residents were, for a while, unaware. Whistler caught one rat drinking from the stream, and after that he kept a look-out for them, both there and by the Pond. He caught two more by the Pond and the Pond then became a favourite patrol area for him. He ignored the young frogs and toads who were growing quickly in the warm water. He waited for larger prey. And it was in this way that the rats' increasing numbers were discovered.

Whistler passed on his discovery to Owl. 'You can profit by this,' he told her. 'You and Hollow.'

'Thanks,' Owl replied. 'That's good news.'

But it wasn't, of course. It was the worst possible news. The rats were grabbing territory where they liked, pushing out mice and shrews on land, and competing with water-voles along the stream. By the Pond, Toad watched them swamping the Edible Frogs' ancient home. And the other Farthing Wood animals saw worrying signs of the rats' determination to colonize every nook and cranny. All the residents were alarmed at the way they were losing ground to the invaders right across the Park. The more timid animals ran before this tide of rodents which seemed about to engulf them.

Fox, Vixen, Weasel, Badger and the birds tried desperately to keep the rats out of their own little corner. But there was a limit to the number they could devour and they couldn't hold back the flood. When their special meeting-place became a nest for a party of rats, it was time to take stock.

'It's war,' Weasel said simply. 'We need to fight to keep what's ours.'

'You mean win back,' Adder corrected her. 'We've already lost the area.'

'Not completely,' Fox said as they sat by his earth. 'We still have our own homes.'

'Just let them try entering my sett,' Badger growled. 'They'll turn themselves into my larder if they do. But what about Mole? Could he defend himself?'

No-one had seen Mossy. 'His best plan is to stay in his tunnels deep underground,' Fox said.

'Can't leave it to chance,' Badger argued. 'I must go and make sure he's all right.'

'When are we going to teach these rodents a lesson?' Weasel snarled. 'We should drive them out of our rendezvous for a start.'

'We'll begin tonight,' Fox answered her. 'We'll round up all our friends and relatives. Then we'll descend on the rats in the dead of night. We won't leave one alive in this neck of the woods if I have anything to do with it.'

'Bravo! That's our Fox talking!' cried Weasel.

Adder's red eyes glittered. 'Just like old times,' she drawled.

CHAPTER EIGHT

Fox led the Farthing Wood fighters towards their traditional meeting place of the Hollow. Any rat that crossed their path as they went along was slain at once. In the Hollow the rats who had settled there sensed danger. They scurried into their burrows and cowered nervously.

Fox knew where their nests were. He began to dig with his front paws. Vixen helped him. Badger used his powerful claws to unearth the rats who shot out of their holes in all directions. The foxes pounced. Weasel snapped. Badger snarled. Twelve rats were killed. More escaped. But the friends were pleased with their work.

'The Hollow's ours again,' said Vixen.

'And will remain so,' Fox stressed. 'But this is only the start. We'll hound those rats and chase them – yes, and slaughter them wherever we find them. Come on, my friends. Let's sweep them away!'

While Fox's band were clearing the home woodland, another of his friends was trying to defend a different area from the invaders. At the Pond, Toad had watched in horror as the bold Bully and his comrades swarmed into the neighbourhood. These rats plunged into the water and swam to the little islet where the Edible Frogs liked to gather. The frogs dived for cover to the pond bottom, but many were caught before they could get away. They were good to eat and the rats bit them greedily, killing or maiming them. Bully took the best pieces first without argument.

The young froglets and toadlets, so recently grown from tadpoles in the pond, panicked. They jumped from the water in a sort of explosion, landing in heaps everywhere. The Farthing Wood Toad saw the rats pounce on the mass, gobbling them horribly. His stout old heart swelled with pity for his relatives' plight. He couldn't fight the rats. He had no sharp teeth or claws. But he cried out in fury at the destruction.

'Villains! Butchers!' he croaked loudly, hopping towards the seething waters. 'How dare you come to this place and ruin our peace? You're not fit to live amongst us. Vicious, poisonous creatures! Leave those frogs alone! This is *their* home! The Warden himself protects – ' his voice ended on a choke as a powerful rat gripped him from behind. Toad struggled in vain.

Bully, sitting on the centre islet, scanned the shore for the cause of the noise. 'Who has the nerve to question us?' he asked roughly.

Toad was silent. He felt the rat's teeth in his neck. Bully's comrade explained.

'A toad?' Bully whispered in disbelief. 'This I must see for myself.' He scrambled into the water and quickly paddled to the bank. He saw the victim who had dared to protest. The rat who had seized Toad had now abruptly let go as the foul taste of Toad's skin – his only defence – got to work.

'Who are you?' Bully asked with a horrible grin, showing his sharp yellow teeth.

'The Farthing Wood Toad,' came the gasping reply.

'Oh. Oh yes,' Bully sneered. 'I've heard of you lot. You clever animals who came here all in a group, helping each other on the way. You're well known all around, aren't you? But I don't see your friends around now, coming to your aid.'

'They'll come,' Toad croaked defiantly.

'Too late, I fear,' Bully leered. 'And there's more of us. *We* like to work together too, don't we, Brat?' He turned to his companion.

'Yes, Bully.'

'We need a proper home too,' Bully continued. 'And now we've got one, we'll settle here for good. We may upset some of you.' He cackled. 'We *are* grubby and hungry. But there's nothing poisonous about us. We're as healthy as anyone. And we want the best for ourselves. Now, you can't blame us for that. So you'll find out now what happens to creatures who object to our ways.'

'Your threats mean nothing to me,' Toad croaked. 'I'm old and helpless. You'll gain very little from attacking me.'

'You'll be a lesson to others,' Bully sneered.

'How will you tackle foxes and badgers?' Toad challenged him.

'We'll overwhelm them! We're quick to multiply. More of us are coming all the time. The Park will teem with rats,' he squealed triumphantly.

Toad sank back, exhausted, aghast at the horrible events Bully was predicting. Dimly he saw a blur of white approaching from a distance. Deer were coming to drink. Even they would find themselves strangers in their own Park if Bully's words became reality.

'Shall I kill him?' Brat growled.

'No. You leave him to me,' Bully answered. '*I* want this one.'

Toad waited for the expected snap of the big rat's jaws. He was unable to move. He was calm and only regretted that he wouldn't see his dear friends again. Bully's gleaming eyes stared at him wickedly.

There was a sound of many feet. The herd of deer, alarmed by the mass of rats all around, had begun to run. They headed for the Pond. Some of the rats were trampled or kicked in the rush. Bully looked up at the towering white beasts. With a final vicious lunge at poor Toad, he scuttled away.

At dawn the next day Whistler flew to the Pond to

catch himself a breakfast. He found no rats, but frog carcasses were lying everywhere. The heron guessed at once who their killers were and began to search frantically for Toad.

'The rats did it! The rats did it!' one of the water-fowl called to Whistler. 'They tried to drive us all out. Only the deer stopped them.'

'Did you see a toad – you know, the old one, who's my friend?' the heron asked worriedly.

'I know the one,' the moorhen answered. 'He's a brave creature. He tried to stop the killing.'

Whistler was filled with pride. How typical of Toad and all the Farthing Wood animals. 'Did he . . . suffer at all?' he hardly dared to ask.

'I'd be surprised if he's still alive,' the moorhen replied sadly, 'when you see what happened to the frogs.'

The tall heron began a fresh search amongst the reeds and sedges. He dreaded what he would find. Toad had managed to crawl under cover but was too weak to call. At last Whistler came near.

'Here!' Toad gasped.

The heron hurried forward and found his little friend badly wounded and scarred. 'Oh Toad, poor, poor, fellow,' he groaned. 'What have they done to you?'

'Made . . . a mess of me.'

Whistler examined him closely. 'You're in a terrible state,' he said miserably. 'I must help you. But – '

'Take me to the Hollow,' Toad whispered. 'Before the . . . rats come back.'

'Of course, of course. Anything. But, Toad, dear friend, would you be able to stand the pain? My bill, you know . . .'

'Better your bill than . . . a rat's fangs,' Toad murmured.

Now Whistler didn't hesitate. As gently as he could, he clasped the little animal in his bill. If he had been gentle with Weasel, now it was as though he was carrying an egg. Toad made no sound. Whistler flew high and slow to the Hollow. He placed Toad amongst some soft vegetation. Then he tossed the dead rats from the meeting-place in a fury.

'Dear Toad, how do you feel?' he asked wretchedly.

There was no reply.

'Toad! Can't you speak, old fellow?'

'Thank you,' Toad whispered, 'for rescuing me.' He gave a long sigh. Then he croaked, 'Tell the others I'm proud to have . . .' His voice died away. Whistler watched in misery as the brave animal gave up the fight. Toad, the discoverer of White Deer Park and the animals' guide during their long journey there, was dead.

CHAPTER NINE

It was a mournful group of animals from Farthing Wood who gathered after Whistler's distressing news. They stood silently in the Hollow, lost in their own thoughts, as they gazed on their old companion.

'How small he looks,' Adder murmured. 'How soft and defenceless. He never seemed to me like that when he was alive. I wish I had been spared this sight.'

'If only he had been captured by the humans, he would have been taken well out of reach of rats,' Weasel said.

'The men were after larger game,' Owl pointed out.

'Why isn't the Warden around?' Leveret demanded. 'We need protection.'

'He has his hands full with the new reserve,' Fox told him. 'There's a nasty surprise waiting for him here.'

'Warden or no Warden, White Deer Park must be saved,' Badger declared. 'We must fight and fight.'

'We must concentrate on our own corner,' Fox

117

said. 'The rats won't be able to regroup in our territory. As soon as they come near, we must strike and keep on striking. We will all stick together and defend one another.'

The animals were buoyed up by this comforting thought. They left the Hollow sadly but determined that no more of their number should suffer Toad's fate. Vixen was the last to leave. She tenderly nosed Toad's body into a clump of fern and scraped some dead leaves around him until he was hidden.

'Whoever caused you to suffer,' she murmured, 'will regret it. You'll be avenged, I promise.'

Badger now headed for the woodland where he had once had his sett. Mossy still lived close to it and Badger wanted to make sure the little mole was all right. The tree which had toppled in the storm and crushed his old home still lay where it had fallen. Badger looked at it and shivered. 'I'm lucky to be alive,' he muttered to himself. 'I'm so ancient I sometimes wonder how I've managed to survive so long.'

One of the sett's entrances was unblocked. He pushed his way in and began to call for Mossy whose tunnels and passages connected here.

'Mole! Mole! It's Badger! Are you there?' He paused to listen. After more calling the scrabbling sound of Mossy's paws could be heard.

'Badger!' the little creature cried joyfully as he smelt, rather than saw his old friend.

'Now, Mole, you shouldn't come looking for intruders,' Badger scolded him. 'I might have been a rat.'

Mossy tittered. 'You a rat? That's silly. I knew it was you. I could smell your scent.'

'Very well. But in future you must keep yourself hidden. Rats are so cunning and nosy. Give 'em a chance, they'll just barge in. You must block up this hole straight away.'

'If you say so, Badger.'

'You can't be too careful. How about food? Are you all right for that?'

'Worms galore,' Mossy answered.

'That's good. You can lie low then. I wanted to make sure you understand the danger we're all in.'

'Thank you, Badger. Will you come again when the danger's passed?'

Badger hesitated. He didn't know when *that* was likely to be. 'I'll be back when the time is right. I can't say more than that just now.'

'I understand,' Mossy replied. 'Badger, do look after yourself too.'

'Of course I will. You can count on that. You know me – I'm a stayer.'

Satisfied that Mossy was safe, Badger hastened back to join the others. The foxes, young and old, were hunting in a group, Weasel told him. 'The rats are on the run here. They can't get away quickly enough.'

Badger noticed blood on Weasel's flanks. 'You're wounded!' he exclaimed. 'Is it bad, Weasel?'

No, no,' she assured him. 'You can't fight without getting a few scratches and bites, you know. I had three rats hanging on me while I dealt with another one.'

'Did you kill them all?'

'You bet I killed them,' Weasel snarled.

'Good. There's no-one like you for a scrap. And I want to play my part in this.'

'Be careful,' Weasel said. 'You're not as nimble as you once were.'

'I still have my teeth,' Badger joked. 'That's all I need.'

Over the next few days the Farthing Wood animals continued to drive the rats from their home area. Those not slain by the foxes, Badger or Weasel were pounced on as they ran by Owl and Hollow. Whistler too, with the thought of Toad never far from his mind, became a great ratter. He patrolled the stream's banks to keep the watercourse free. Adder and her mate Sinuous slid into the nests of nursing female rats and gobbled up their young. Every baby rat removed now was one less adult to menace the Park in the future.

And it wasn't only the Farthing Wood band who battled to save themselves and their territory. Throughout the Reserve the hunting beasts and birds were on the attack. Yet it seemed that, as fast as they cleared one colony of rats from their midst, another appeared in its place. It was as though all the rats from miles around were clustering to snatch White Deer Park from the rightful inhabitants.

After the capture and removal of animals to the new enclosure, the Warden was keen to see how they settled down there and where they were making their homes. Every day Plucky saw him on his rounds. The young fox became used to the pattern, and he started to think about it. He listened for the noise of the Land Rover's engine. He knew the tall wooden gates would be opened, the vehicle driven through, the gates shut behind it. A cattle grid prevented animals escaping through the open gates, but Plucky didn't concern himself with that. He thought that if one machine could carry him *into* the enclosure, another could just as easily carry him out. He began to watch the Warden's movements closely, never straying far from a screen of vegetation near the double gates. He noticed each time the man had to turn the vehicle after his tour of inspection before driving home. He thought this manoeuvre offered him a chance. There was a way into the vehicle through the back, which was open. If he could get inside, the Warden would do the rest for him!

One morning he was ready to try his luck. He longed to see Dash and all his other friends again who he felt had forgotten him. He lay low in a ditch as the familiar hum of the car engine approached. And there he stayed, on tenterhooks, while the Warden made his tour. Only when the man returned, much later, and got into the Land Rover again did Plucky stir. As the vehicle began its turn he crept forward. Then, as the rear of the Land Rover swung round, he began to run. He knew it was now or never. The vehicle moved off. Plucky jumped up and, taking a flying leap, crashed inside the back of it, sprawling on top of an assortment of objects. The fox, shocked and badly winded, had one huge piece of luck. The noise and jolt of his landing was deadened by the loud rattling of the wheels as they crossed the cattle grid. The Warden was completely unaware of his passenger. He stopped the car to open the gates. Plucky flattened himself against the floor. In a moment he was outside the enclosure again. The gates were closed and the Land Rover continued on its way. Plucky bounded free and half fell, half rolled on to the downland turf. Bruised but otherwise unhurt, he set off at once for the boundary fence of White Deer Park as the Warden's car disappeared.

He found Dash's scrape and scrambled through, then ran straight to the favourite spot where he and the young hare had played together. Plucky called excitedly. Dash was nowhere near and Plucky only succeeded in waking Owl who was dozing in the sunshine.

'Yap, yap, it's always the same with you young-sters,' the bird complained. 'No consideration.'

'Owl!' Plucky cried joyfully. 'It's me, Plucky! Don't you recognize me?'

Owl peered down. 'Plucky? But you – I mean, how did you – '

'Escape?' Plucky finished. 'By the wit and cunning I inherited. It's marvellous to see you and know I'm back with all my friends. Is Dash safe?'

'Yes, she's safe,' Owl replied. 'But the Park has been overrun by rats. And one of our number, a dear old friend, hasn't survived.'

'Who? Who?' Plucky yelped.

'Toad. He was attacked and couldn't defend himself. He died bravely. The rest of us have declared war on the rat hordes.'

'Poor harmless, good-hearted Toad,' Plucky murmured sorrowfully. 'He never threatened a soul. I'll join the fight,' he added grimly. 'Have you caught rats?'

'Heaps,' Owl replied. 'I eat almost nothing else.'

'You certainly look well fed,' was Plucky's comment as they travelled together to the home area.

Fox and Vixen were overwhelmed by Plucky's return and listened enthralled as he related how he had managed to escape.

'A very clever idea,' Fox said with admiration. 'I congratulate you.'

Plucky was restless and made his excuses.

'No need to guess who you want to see,' Vixen commented. 'She's bound to be nearby.'

Plucky loped away, full of high spirits.

'A fox and a hare,' Owl murmured. 'A strange sort of friendship. It could only happen amongst Farthing Wood animals.'

'On the contrary, they're White Deer Park animals through and through,' Fox pointed out. 'Farthing Wood is only a name to them.'

'You know what I mean, Fox. The place has gone, but the spirit of it lives on here. And so it will, as long as we keep it alive.'

Fox was moved. 'Oh Owl,' he said. 'It's good to hear that. It puts new heart into me.'

Plucky discovered Dash drowsing in the long grass. He stood and waited for her to awake. A slight breeze blew and she opened her eyes. She was so astonished she leapt high and began to run. Plucky called her back. Dash danced around him, unable to keep still.

'Stop, stop,' he cried in delight. 'My head is spinning.'

'Tell me everything!' she ordered him. '*You* weren't carried out by Whistler.'

'Well, I simply decided to leave that enclosure the same way I entered it.' He described his adventure exactly.

'Brilliant!' she squealed. 'Even Fox himself never

124

thought of that idea. I'm so proud of you, Plucky, and I'm really glad we're friends.'

'We always will be,' he told her. 'We grew up together. One day we'll have our own mates and our own litters, but you and I will always be friends.'

'Yes,' said Dash. 'Friendship like ours really is forever.'

CHAPTER TEN

The rats returned to the Pond. The mass of toadlets and froglets made fine food. Bully smacked his lips as he crunched up the tiny prey.

'There's food to be had everywhere in this place,' he said eagerly, 'if you know where to look. And there's nothing like a rat for digging up a meal.' He looked around at his henchmen. 'Eat well,' he told them. 'We need all our strength. And keep your teeth sharp. The main battle's coming. We still have to deal with the old comrades.'

'Who are they?' a young rat squeaked.

'The very ones who drove our friends out of that wood on the other side of the Park. The fox and the badger, the owl and the weasel – all their hangers-on – we'll show them! There will be such a horde of us soon we'll drown them in bodies.'

The other rats were silent. They weren't so confident. Bully went on, 'We'll advance through the wood, taking a tree at a time. Then we'll climb the trees, up and on to the low branches, see? *And* cling to the trunks where they can't see us. When we're good and thick in the trees we'll drop down on them like wasps on rotten fruit.'

A big rat called Spike said, 'I wouldn't describe those Farthing Wood animals as rotten. Nothing soft about *them*. They're tough and cunning. Look at their leader . . .'

'They're old, all of them,' Bully snapped. 'They've only had our females to fight mostly, so far. It'll be different next time.'

The others weren't convinced. 'It won't be safe up the trees with an owl picking us off,' the young rat complained.

'The owl?' Bully laughed. 'She's got so fat she can hardly fly! Let her catch some more of us – the faint-hearted ones, like you' – he sneered – 'it's all to the good! We'll weigh her down, ha ha! Even dead rats can be useful!' He leered at his astonished listeners. 'And first,' he told them, 'we're going after the snake. She seeks out our weakest. Let's see how she copes with fighting our strongest.'

Adder's loathing of rats was increased by the death of her old companion, Toad. And, as she was so close to the ground, she knew where many of the females had made their nests. She waged a campaign against the females and their young and, with Sinuous alongside her, the pair of snakes were lethal. Bully, however, was about to put a stop to this.

He decided to ambush Adder as she launched an attack. He, Brat, Spike and a number of other males hid themselves in a nest near a mossy bank where Adder loved to sunbathe. The squeaks of tiny rat babies was like a magnet to the snakes. They slithered eagerly through the dry undergrowth.

'Warm pink rats asleep in their den, not knowing that Adder is coming again,' the snake sang to herself.

Sinuous joined in: 'A rat makes a break in the diet of a snake.'

Side by side they slid to the nest where Bully and his followers were waiting. Adder entered first. Her busy forked tongue quickly picked up the odour of the male rats. She froze. There was danger here. She called behind to Sinuous, 'Stay outside! There's a trap for us!'

Sinuous shot away but Adder was caught. She felt two pairs of jaws clamp her in the middle. In the darkness she couldn't see her attackers, but she lunged to left and right, her poison fangs trying to find a mark.

'Hold back,' Bully shrieked. 'There's death in those fangs.'

Other rats were kept at bay but Adder's thin body was held firm by the gripping jaws.

'You've made one visit too many to our nests, Poisonous One,' Bully taunted her. 'You'd murder all our babies, wouldn't you?'

Sinuous darted through leaves and twigs, expecting the rats to be upon him at any moment. He believed Adder to be already dead. He aimed for a large flat rock under which he often hid. In his rush towards his bolt-hole, he slid under the very noses of Plucky and Dash, who were sunning themselves on a high bank overlooking the stream.

Plucky jumped up. 'You're in a hurry,' he barked. He knew the snake was Adder's companion.

'The rats have turned the tables on us,' Sinuous hissed urgently. 'An ambush – back there.'

'Where's Adder?' Plucky demanded.

'I fear it's too late,' Sinuous told him.

'Where is she?' Plucky insisted. 'Dash, run off and get the seniors – any of them. Now' – he turned back to the snake – 'give me directions. Quickly.'

'Go towards the slope and follow it down. Run through the heather to a bare patch of ground where the bracken shoots are uncurling. You'll see a small hole under a patch of bilberry. That's where Adder is.' Sinuous wasted no more time but slithered hastily away.

Plucky sped towards the rat-hole. It was too small for him to enter. The smell of rats was strong. 'Adder!' he called sharply. 'Are you all right? It's me – Plucky. I'm here to help!'

Adder, still bravely ducking and weaving to prevent any more rats seizing her, answered sarcastically, 'I'm certainly not all right. Unless carrying two large rodents on my back with their teeth piercing my skin is a normal state of affairs.'

Plucky dug vigorously into the hole with his front feet, scattering earth behind him. Now and then he raised his head and barked loudly to show others where he was. Soon Plucky could see some of the rats who backed further into the hole.

Bully realized that, with Plucky's arrival, the rats were now at a disadvantage. 'Keep your distance, young fox,' he warned, 'or the snake dies.'

Plucky hesitated. He couldn't yet see Adder. 'Very well,' he replied. 'Let Adder go and I'll come no nearer. But if not, I'll dig you all out!' He turned and barked again. Dash heard his call as she streaked overland for more help. The rats squeaked and squealed in the dark hole as they argued amongst each other.

'Stand back,' Bully suddenly cried, 'so that we know there's no trick.'

Plucky backed a little and Adder, bruised, angry and defiant, emerged from the nest. Her tough scaly skin had proved a barrier to the rats' teeth where Toad's soft hide had not. 'I'm in your debt,' the snake said graciously as Plucky came to examine her. 'No great harm done, except to my dignity.'

'How many attacked you?'

'Two. I managed to keep the others off.'

'Get yourself under cover,' Plucky advised. 'I'll deal with these customers.'

Adder slid gratefully away. Plucky crept back to the hole. The rats were still chattering. Presently Bully came out. Before Plucky could pounce, Bully squealed, 'Listen to a rat just this once. We're animals too, you know. We have our homes and youngsters to look after. The snake came hunting for our babies. What else could we do but try to defend them?'

Plucky said nothing.

'Why can't you and your friends and me and mine come to a sort of pact?' Bully wheedled.

'Are you speaking as the leader of the rat pack?'

'I'm as much the leader as anyone,' Bully replied, grinning. 'Listen, suppose we rats agree not to cross into your particular area? It's a big park; we'll avoid that bit. These constant clashes do nobody any good.'

'I haven't the authority to answer you,' Plucky informed the rat. 'I only know we all object to your coming here and we'd like to be rid of you. But if you refuse to leave, we'll defend our territories as long as necessary.'

'Then you agree to my suggestion?' Bully prompted. 'We leave you alone. You do the same for us.'

'I'm not one of the Farthing Wood elders. They make the decisions about such things. But I can carry your message back to them. I think this kind of truce might be of interest.' Privately he doubted if Fox, Badger and the others would settle for such a limited truce, but it gained time.

'Take the message,' said Bully. 'The arrangement will benefit all of us.' He returned to the nest with a sense of triumph. With the powerful Farthing Wood animals out of the way, the rats had a chance

131

of building up their numbers until even those legendary campaigners couldn't hold them.

Brat, Spike and the rest clustered around him as Plucky left the scene. They demanded to know all the details of his latest feat of cunning. With a wide sly leer Bully told them.

'It's faultless. We can do as we please. That fox and his pals won't touch us for a while. And the other hunters in the Reserve are all a half-hearted lot by comparison. *They* won't stop us. When we've made ourselves supreme, we'll put my plan into operation to defeat the last of the Old Guard' – he referred to the Farthing Wood band – 'and in the meantime, we'll make certain the snake is out of the way. We know where she lurks. The ambush didn't quite come off. So we'll make up a real hunting party. We'll lose no more babies to that reptile's stomach.'

CHAPTER ELEVEN

Plucky's barks brought answering calls from Fox who was running with Dash to find him. Plucky quickly gave them a run-down on what had happened.

'You did well,' Fox told him. 'A truce gives us a breathing space just now when families are raising young. But so it does for the rats. And I know this is only a lull. They'll be back.'

That night the sly rats, knowing the Farthing Wood animals' guard was down, set off swiftly for Adder's haunt. They hoped to catch her asleep. Their scurrying noises awoke Sinuous under his flat rock. He thought he was hearing mice noises and slid into the open. He was hungry. He hadn't seen Adder since the ambush and had no way of knowing that she had escaped. The rats, bunched together, rushed forward. One snake was as much like another to their eyes. Brat and Spike were in the forefront. Sinuous realized his error. He struck at Brat and his fangs pierced him through. But while his jaws were locked he was seized by Bully and his comrades. Eight rats held him to the ground, gnawing horribly at his body. This time they would make no mistake as they thought they had Adder at their mercy. Sinuous was unable to squirm, clamped fast in the rats' jaws. The life ebbed out of him. Even then the rats held fast until at last they were quite sure he was dead.

'She'll trouble us no more,' Bully snarled. 'Our babies are safe.' He cared nothing for Brat's carcass. The deed was done. 'We'll leave this area now until we have our full strength. The adder's precious friends will find her here and know we're to be reckoned with.'

The other rats mumbled together. Some of them thought Adder's friends might plan a retaliation when her body was found. First the toad, then the snake . . .

'What are you muttering about?' Bully snapped.

'We think the Old Guard will swear vengeance for this,' Spike grumbled.

'What can they do?' Bully challenged him. 'Haven't they agreed to my pact?'

'The young fox said he would pass your message on, nothing else . . .'

'*I* know they'll do nothing,' Bully growled. 'They have broods to feed like us. They need a truce just as much.'

The rats dispersed to their own nests, innocent of the fact that Adder was actually resting by the stream, soothing her wounds underwater.

Badger was another animal glad of a rest. He had ignored his great age during the recent skirmishes. Now, during the lull in fighting, he realized he had done too much. A tremendous weariness overcame him. He was too tired to forage. He sank down inside his sett. 'Oh, what an old fool I am,' he nagged himself. 'I should have known better. How glad I am my home is so close to Fox and Vixen's. I might need their help. But not yet . . . I mustn't bother them unnecessarily . . .' He fell asleep.

Later a stranger, a young female badger, entered the wood, looking for a resting place. She had been driven from her own territory by a vast swarm of rats. She had been brought up in the once deserted sett by the Pond, where the Farthing Wood animals had escaped from Trey. She came to Badger's home and paused. She smelt badger smells and she heard snoring. She could tell only one animal was inside. She was curious and, cautiously, she entered.

Badger lay on his bedding of dry leaves and grass. His own particular smell was recognized by the youngster. She had seen him around and knew he was the Farthing Wood badger, a kindly old creature.

'I know you live alone,' she spoke to him. 'My mother once offered you a share of our sett. You were too proud to accept. Now I'm asking *you* for shelter.'

Eventually Badger sensed her presence. 'Who's there?' he cried.

'A homeless young badger.'

'Oh. Then you must tell me everything. Settle yourself down.'

'You're very kind.'

'Which badger are you?'

She explained, adding, 'My name is Frond.'

'I know the sett you described. And I remember your mother,' Badger said. 'What happened to you?'

'We were driven away by the rats.'

'I understand all about that,' Badger nodded. 'Well, you'll be at peace here for a while. Oh, how tired I am.' He yawned widely. 'Too tired even to collect my food tonight.'

Frond eagerly offered to help. 'I'll bring you something,' she told him. 'It's the least I can do in return for shelter. In fact, while you sleep again, I'll bring enough for a feast!'

While she collected the food, unknown to Frond a pair of onlookers was watching her. Dash and Plucky saw Frond gather the titbits together at the foot of a tree.

'I haven't seen her before,' Dash said.

'No. I wonder what she's going to do with all that food?' Plucky muttered.

They watched a while longer. Frond took a knot of worms in her mouth and went towards Badger's sett. The friends were alarmed as they saw her enter.

'Where's Badger? Plucky cried. 'He can't have gone. He hasn't . . .' He dared not voice his thoughts. They ran to the sett. Frond was returning for more food.

'Where's Badger?' Where is he?' Dash shrilled.

Frond backed nervously. 'He's inside. Munching worms. He's all right, really.'

'So that food is for him?'

'Yes.' Frond explained the situation. 'Are you Farthing Wood animals?' she asked shyly.

'No. White Deer Park born and bred. But related. Well,' he added, looking at her admiringly, 'Badger should consider himself lucky.'

'I'm only too happy to help,' Frond assured him. 'He's exhausted himself.'

'Well, give the dear old fellow our greetings,' Plucky said. 'Tell him Plucky and Dash look forward to seeing him back amongst us.'

'Plucky and Dash,' Frond repeated. 'Nice names.'

'And what's yours?' Dash enquired.

'Frond. I hope we may be friends?'

'I hope so too,' said Plucky. 'Come on, Dash. Let's have a game.'

CHAPTER TWELVE

Weasel found the dry remains of Sinuous under the flat rock. She told her friends who could only wonder at Adder's feelings. 'The rats probably think they killed *her*,' Fox remarked grimly. 'So much for their pact!'

The Farthing Wood animals held themselves ready in the lull for the expected showdown. Each of them were prepared to fight to the bitter end. Better to die than be holed up in a corner of the Reserve by a sea of greedy, dangerous invaders.

At last the day came. Bully roused his mass of followers. He was eager for battle. 'We strike by night into territory of the old comrades.'

'The Old Guard?' Spike gasped.

'You heard me!' Bully snapped. 'And let me stress the word "old" once again. Because that's certainly what they are!'

'All of them?' Spike dared to ask.

Bully ignored him. 'We're at full strength now,' he continued. 'We'll mass together and run for their corner. Wave after wave of us. We'll swarm up the trees. We'll carpet the ground. By tonight the old fogies will be overthrown.'

Under cover of darkness the rats grouped. Bully took the lead. Like ripples on water, the rodents moved silently towards their goal. They reached the first trees on the outskirts of the woodland where Bully believed the Farthing Wood animals had their homes. He directed some of the smaller males to scale these trees so that, as the biggest, strongest animals penetrated deep inside the wood, they would have their rear guarded. Some rats swarmed up the trunks, lying low along the branches. Others clung to the trunks themselves. From here they would drop on anything that moved below.

The main body of fighters pressed on, meeting no resistance.

'You sure this is the place?' Spike grunted in surprise.

Bully snarled at him. But even he was doubtful. Where *were* the Farthing Wood animals?

Suddenly another big male hissed, 'I see movement ahead!'

The rats came to a halt in dead silence. Hundreds of pairs of eyes pierced the darkness. A mole scurried through the leaf litter.

'Kill it!' Bully commanded.

Spike ran forward. Mossy – for it was he – spun round. He had been in quest of food. He squealed in terror. Spike quickly cut short his cry. Poor helpless Mossy was felled, but not before an owl, coasting aloft, saw it happen. Hollow, the male owl, saw the massed ranks of rats and veered away to give the warning. Bully had led his army into the storm-damaged wood where Badger had once had his sett. Mossy's home was there, but most of his friends now gathered in the neighbouring copse where Fox and Vixen had their earth. Hollow flew straight to Owl. 'They're coming!' he screeched. 'The rats are coming in force!'

Owl heaved her bulk into the air, calling, repeatedly, 'Make ready! The enemy is approaching!'

Fox, Vixen and Weasel rushed to the point chosen as their first line of defence. This was a thick stand of holly scrub, almost impenetrable. They sheltered behind it, looking out over open ground which the rats would have to cross. The other foxes came running – Friendly, Charmer, Plucky and all their relations. Dash and her father, Whistler and Adder joined them, some for support, some for protection. Frond emerged from Badger's sett and stood before it, determined to defend the old creature.

Mossy's death had goaded the rats into a mad rush forward which Bully couldn't check. Still they were unchallenged and the rush carried them far into the wood. Bully knew he had miscalculated where the battle would happen. Yet he couldn't hold back the mass movement. The rats posted amongst the branches were left behind, not knowing they were in the wrong place.

The army passed on like a flood. Bully vainly tried to halt them. The element of surprise was lost. The Farthing Wood animals listened tensely to the patter of a thousand rat feet.

'We can catch them in the rear,' Owl hooted to Hollow and Whistler. 'Come on, let's pick them off.' They sped over the tree-tops. Hollow knew the way.

'There!' he screeched. Owl gasped as she saw the living tide of rats. Each owl pinpointed an animal and swooped down, talons at the ready. Time and time again they dived, impaling a rat and flying upwards again to drop it from a height. Whistler used different tactics. His weapon was his bill. He stood at the side of the mass and stabbed repeatedly as the rats poured past. The rodents were so tightly packed that they had no defence from the attackers. Yet the birds were barely able to make a dent in the horde. The rats swept on to the open ground.

The waiting Farthing Wood band saw with horror the task that faced them. The lines of invaders stretched out into the distance.

'We'll fight to the end,' Fox said quietly. 'We'll save our homes or die in the attempt.'

Bully and Spike got themselves out of the headlong rush as the leading rats crashed against the screen of holly. There were shrieks of pain as the sharp prickles tore their skin. The foxes snapped as each rodent tried to force a way through. Weasel, a furious fighter, attacked three animals at once. Now the battle began in earnest.

The rats opened up gaps in the holly and poured through. They hurled themselves in clusters at the group of friends. Foxes, owls, hedgehogs, Weasel, Adder and Whistler fought tooth, beak and claw. Many rats were crushed, but soon the friends were close to being overwhelmed. Their bodies were covered by scratching, biting rodents. They tossed them aside, but new ones took their place. Now Frond ran forward to help. Badger, hearing the din outside, lumbered to his sett exit. His friends were sorely pressed. How could he remain outside the fight? He didn't wish to survive if his friends perished. The rats poured over him too.

Dash and her father raced away from the scene. They had one thought in their minds: to rouse the rest of the Park's residents, deer herd and every other willing creature, to come to the rescue, to fight side by side to save the Nature Reserve. Dash soon left her father far behind. Both the hares spread the message, and both gathered help.

The entire population of the Reserve had been affected by the rats' menace. Now animals gathered in groups, rallying to the cry. Dash roused the white deer, the largest of all the creatures of the Park. The herd, stags leading, trotted forward, then broke into a canter. More and more animals joined the throng.

Meanwhile the rats were gaining control. Bully saw the fight was nearly over. The foxes twisted and turned as they snapped and lunged wearily. Adder was buried under a score of rodents as she tried to bury her fangs into Spike. Weasel was down, on her back, kicking and biting at her attackers. Only Frond was fairly fresh. Even the birds' swoops were weakening. They began to see the end was approaching. Badger still fought, thinking each breath might be his last.

But suddenly the other animals called up by Dash and Leveret burst upon the scene. The deer trampled the carpet of rats as they galloped forward. They turned and pounded over them again. For the first time the rats fell back. Adder emerged once more into the open and slid out of the path of the deer hoofs. Now the deer lowered their antlers and swept up the rodents, tossing them into the air. The rats thudded down, bruised or maimed. Dozens squirmed on the ground, crushed by hoofs. The other forces of animals brought in from outside pitched in too. Bully saw the tide begin to turn.

The Farthing Wood group took new heart and found a fresh strength to fight. Owl darted down to rescue Weasel from her attackers. The foxes flung the rats from their bodies. Bully was squealing orders to retreat before all were killed. The rats were pummelled on all sides. Spike was at last brought down by Adder who slew him with an accompanying hiss: 'Ssin-u-ouss.'

Fox sought out Bully himself. The big rat was scuttling away. Fox gave chase but Vixen was ahead of him. She remembered her solemn vow to Toad. She grabbed Bully and snatched him up in her jaws. Then she ran away from the battleground. Bully struggled in vain. Vixen, followed by Fox, ran for the boundary fence. She clenched her jaws tighter, tighter . . . The helpless Bully was crushed between them. Vixen shook him like a terrier and hurled his carcass over the fence beyond White Deer Park.

Fox watched her grimly. 'The others will follow,' he growled.

CHAPTER THIRTEEN

The victorious White Deer Park animals drove the rats before them. The rodents gave up the fight and ran back to the wood where their comrades still clung to the branches they had climbed. These rats had listened to the sounds of battle and were waiting only to drop down on their enemies as they were chased under the trees by Bully and his triumphant troops. So when the defeated rats came running underneath, the ambushers automatically dropped on them and began to fight viciously. Rat fought rat in the darkness and many were killed before they realized what was happening.

Fox and Vixen rushed back to the side of their allies who were pursuing what was left of the rodent horde. Only Adder and Badger stayed behind on the battlefield.

'Well, we survived,' said Adder. 'How I have come to hate the sight of a rat!'

'Sight and smell,' Badger muttered, looki around at the heaped bodies. 'Their odour is gusting.'

The rat carcasses made a trail through the P

the boundary fence. Mossy's body was hidden beneath a pile of rodents. So his death, unlike Toad's, was kept a secret from his friends. The survivors amongst the rat invaders bolted under the Park's fence, desperate to escape to the familiar dark tunnels of the sewer system they had spread from. In an hour not one remained within the Reserve they had set out to conquer.

The residents, weary but joyful, returned to their homes. Dawn broke over the Park. Birds cried happily. The Farthing Wood animals could only now see the full extent of the slaughter.

'This is an ugly mess,' Fox remarked.

'The Warden will take care of things,' Badger said, 'when he's recovered from the shock.'

There were, of course, other deaths apart from those of the rats. Vixen said, 'We're lucky that more of us weren't killed.' She thought of Toad in particular.

Now Badger recalled his little friend Mossy. 'We haven't seen Mole,' he murmured, looking puzzled. 'Where's Mole?'

There was a silence. No-one knew. The animals looked distressed, guessing some accident must have befallen him. Why else wouldn't he have joined them?

'Perhaps he's still underground?' Badger faltered. 'I told him to stay there. But he couldn't . . . stay there always. Could he?' He glanced at the others sorrowfully. None of his friends could offer any

146

hope. 'I must discover the truth,' Badger murmured. 'When I'm not so weary I'll . . . I'll . . .' His voice faded.

'You need to rest,' Frond whispered. 'Let me help you back.'

'Dear Badger,' Fox said affectionately. 'Frond, you must tend him. Badger has proved once again how much we need him.'

The old creature allowed himself to be led back to his sett. He was tired beyond belief.

'Do you think he'll recover?' Whistler asked anxiously.

'On his own, maybe not,' Vixen murmured. 'But he has Frond to look after him now. She'll make a great difference.'

As the friends dispersed, Weasel ran to Owl. 'I haven't thanked you properly,' she said. 'You saved me.'

'Oh well, I could see you were in difficulties . . .' Owl replied awkwardly.

'It was all up with me,' Weasel insisted. 'Let's make a new start, shall we? I don't know why we always niggled each other. Let's be proper friends from now on.'

'Weasel, I should like that. I really should.'

Later that morning the Warden saw the bloodbath that had taken place overnight. Badger had been right – he could scarcely believe his eyes. It was obvious a tremendous battle had taken place. The man could only wonder at the extraordinary alliance that must have been formed amongst the Park's inhabitants to defeat the invaders. He quickly organized a clearance of the unsavoury piles of rats.

And now there was a surprise for the animals too. Whistler noticed men putting up a new fence around part of the downland between White Deer Park and the new walled enclosure. He kept his eyes on the men's progress over the following days. When the fence was finished the men made an opening in the wall that had enclosed Plucky and Weasel as well as many other animals. At the other end a section of the boundary fence of White Deer Park was removed. Before the heron could grasp what was happening Dash, on one of her madcap runs, found she could race directly on to the downland. There was no need for a scrape to be dug any more. She pelted back to tell her father.

'Come and see,' she begged him. 'Come and see how far we can go.'

Her father was cautious. 'Plenty of time,' he replied. 'I think we should tell the others first.'

'You tell them,' Dash said impatiently. 'I know one animal who will go with me.'

Plucky came to her calls. He was excited by Dash's news. The two playmates ran together and, to their amazement, were able to run right into the second Reserve where Plucky had once been trapped. The two parks were joined together! The animals couldn't know about the complicated human dealings that had brought about this astonishing event, but they did understand that the two reserves were now joined as one. All the animals were in one new White Deer Park, almost twice as large as before.

Between them Whistler, Plucky and Dash spread the news. Soon those friends, taken from the original Reserve because of overcrowding, were free to return to their old homes. Some did. Some didn't. It didn't matter any more. Everyone was free to explore the new territory and to enjoy the extra space. The Farthing Wood animals went to look at the new area. Only Badger showed little interest. The distance was too great for him.

Frond described what she had seen.

'I understand,' Badger said. 'But, you know, Frond, there can never be anywhere better than this dear familiar spot. It's as though we brought our own little piece of Farthing Wood with us.'

Other great reads ⤝ *from* **Red Fox**

Further Red Fox titles that you might enjoy reading are listed on the following pages. They are available in bookshops or they can be ordered directly from us.

If you would like to order books, please send this form and the money due to:

ARROW BOOKS, BOOKSERVICE BY POST, PO BOX 29, DOUGLAS, ISLE OF MAN, BRITISH ISLES. Please enclose a cheque or postal order made out to Arrow Books Ltd for the amount due, plus 75p per book for postage and packing to a maximum of £7.50, both for orders within the UK. For customers outside the UK, please allow £1.00 per book.

NAME _____

ADDRESS _____

_____

Please print clearly.

Whilst every effort is made to keep prices low, it is sometimes necessary to increase cover prices at short notice. If you are ordering books by post, to save delay it is advisable to phone to confirm the correct price. The number to ring is THE SALES DEPARTMENT 071 (if outside London) 973 9700.

Animal Action from Colin Dann

There's much more to Colin Dann than Farthing Wood, as all of these great animal stories prove!

THE BEACH DOGS

Lively mongrel Jack persuades Zoe and Bertram to leave their dull shorebound lives behind and escape to a remote island.

ISBN 0 09 961380 8   £2.99

KING OF THE VAGABONDS

Sammy is a daring cat who'll stop at nothing in order to satisfy his curiosity. And hunting with the Vagabonds – a horde of wild cats – means that life is always full of danger and excitement.

ISBN 0 09 957190 0   £2.99

THE CITY CATS

Out scavenging for food, Sammy and his companion Pinkie find themselves trapped in a delivery van, speeding towards an unknown destination and a terrifying new life.

ISBN 0 09 993890 1   £2.99

THE RAM OF SWEETRIVER

The Sweetriver flock has survived the terrible storm which destroyed their valley. But can they survive the long journey to new pastures?

ISBN 0 09 951240 8   £2.99

JUST NUFFIN

Nuffin – the abandoned puppy who's no more than skin and bone – transforms the Spencer family's holiday from the start. Roger desperately wants to keep him, and Dad definitely doesn't . . .

ISBN 0 09 966900 5   £2.99

A GREAT ESCAPE

Eric made up his mind. He would go to the pet shop, open the cages and let all the animals free to make their own way in the world . . .

ISBN 0 09 977150 0   £2.99

The Farthing Wood Series

Six novels about the animals who live in the White Deer Park nature reserve. Now a successful animated television series.

IN THE GRIP OF WINTER

In the depths of winter, with snow deep on the ground and food scarce, Badger lies alone and injured. No one knows where he is and the frost is tightening its grip every second . . .

ISBN 0 09 929220 3   £2.99

FOX'S FEUD

The fox cub Dreamer has been killed in an attack by the old fox, Scarface, who feels threatened by the new arrivals in White Deer Park. Fox vows revenge, but will he meet his match in Scarface?

ISBN 0 09 920521 1   £2.99

THE FOX CUB BOLD

Bold has left the reserve in search of adventure, which he finds, until he is wounded by a hunter's bullet and left alone, and injured.

ISBN 0 09 920531 9   £2.99

THE SIEGE OF WHITE DEER PARK

Terror has come to White Deer Park. A killer beast is loose, taking lives silently, skilfully and with no trace. Can the Farthing Wood animals stop the beast, before it's their turn?

ISBN 0 09 944760 6   £2.99

IN THE PATH OF THE STORM

Trey, leader of the deer, decides that there is no room for smaller animals in the reserve. The future looks bleak for Adder and the others – and the great storm brings yet more danger.

ISBN 0 09 920551 3   £2.99

BATTLE FOR THE PARK

Not only is the Warden of White Deer Park suddenly removing animals from the reserve, but a colony of rats have invaded and are taking over! There's only one thing for it: war . . .

ISBN 0 09 999690 1   £2.99